Someday Belongs to Us

MARGIE SEAMAN

StoneyCreekPublishing.com

Cover and interior design by TLC Book Design
TLCBookDesign.com
Cover: Monica Thomas, Interior: Erin Stark

Cover illustration, images from Adobe Stock: cruise ship ©Maridav, time warp ©Kirsty Pargeter, Brigantine ship ©Levgen Malamud, starry sky ©Inga Av, ocean ©Mykola Mazuryk

Softcover: 978-1-7368390-7-2
Hardcover: 978-1-7368390-9-6
Ebook: 978-1-7368390-8-9
Library of Congress Control Number: 2022905277

StoneyCreekPublishing.com

To all my brothers and sisters in age,
I dedicate this book as proof that goals
can be reached at any age in life.

Chapter One

$\mathcal{K}$ate Caldwell paced around her office, cell phone pressed to her ear, and alternated between staring at her black Michael Kors pumps on the carpet and her tall picture window. She heard the front door of her home open, a sign that her granddaughter Ellie had arrived.

"Sally, I know we need to move ahead on the new book," Kate told her editor. "I'm trying but the words aren't coming. I'm fighting a complete writer's block. Nothing is working. And now, while I'm trying to deal with that, you call to tell me that not only do I need to hurry up with the book, but I also need to spice up the love scenes! I don't understand. For thirty years, my success has come from writing novels about romance and love—not pornography! My characters are not the type to indulge in just the casual, headboard-banging sex that seems so popular these days. My readers want the real thing. They don't want some hot sheets hotel quickie encounter. They want love!"

"Kate, we have years and years of market research. I respect you as a writer, but you have to listen to what the focus groups are saying," Sally said.

Kate grew more frustrated by the minute. She heard Ellie walking on the hardwood floors for a moment before the footsteps stopped. She had probably found a seat on the oversized tufted bench in the foyer as she always did when she waited for Kate to finish working.

"Please tell me how these focus groups could possibly consider burning loins and body parts that throb and pulsate to be romance? That sounds more like demonic possession complete with head-spinning and throwing up green pea soup!"

At seventy-two, Kate had written more than thirty romance novels under the nom de plume Desiree Desire, with most of them reaching bestseller status. Her last two books captured the escapades of a swash-buckling pirate named Captain Edward Peregrine, captain of his ship, the *Falcon*. He had rakish good looks and romantic dalliances that captivated the hearts of thousands of women readers, both young and old. The readers had faithfully awaited every new seagoing adventure and amorous antic of their favorite hero.

However, it had been almost a year since the second book was published. Both her editor and her loyal fans were growing impatient for the next story. Unfortunately, she had been experiencing a creative slowdown and a lack of inspiration that made starting the new book impossible.

"Society has changed since the 1950s," Sally replied. "People aren't afraid to talk about sex anymore. They want it normalized, and the best way to do that is to include it in normal portrayals of relationships. If you're going to write romance stories about people falling in love, those people are going to have sex. Unless you're suddenly going to write for the Christian romance market."

Thinking of her granddaughter, Kate walked over to the office door and waved to Ellie as a signal that Kate knew she'd arrived. Ellie smiled and waved back, then returned to tapping on the screen of her phone.

"I know. I know. The Internet has changed the world. People don't have time for love any more. Okay, I'll think about it, but I've got to go now. Ellie just came in. We are leaving in the morning. I've still got a million things to do. Who knows, maybe I'll get lucky and meet someone on the cruise who will sweep me off my feet and give me some ideas on just what constitutes spicy sex." Laughing at the absurd idea of finding a potential lover this late in her life, Kate hung up the phone.

She turned to the mahogany-framed mirror hanging on the wall next to her, studying her features. When she first started writing thirty years ago, her hair was still blond. Her wrinkles weren't quite as prominent, and the dark spots of age hadn't made their appearance on her hands.

Now there she stood, the epitome of a strong, mature Texas woman. Kate took pride in the fact that she always dressed her tall, slim figure in stylish, designer clothes. Today, she wore black, soft wool casual pants topped with a pearl white oversized cashmere sweater. Her thick silver hair was cut in a short wedge.

She turned from her reflection in the mirror to see her granddaughter walking towards her office. Ellie must have heard enough of the conversation to know that Kate had hung up the phone.

Pride filled Kate as she watched Ellie coming down the hall. She remembered that as soon as she was old enough to truly understand that she was a girl and would one day have children, she had been thrilled. Even more exciting was the realization that she would someday be a grandmother! Even as youthful as she looked when her first grandchild was born,

Kate hadn't wanted any of the names women usually picked in lieu of the traditional grandma. She had waited for that day all her life, and she wanted the title.

"Grandma!" Ellie squealed happily as she walked through the doorway. "I came by to see if you need any last-minute things to take on the cruise. I'm going to the mall and can pick up whatever you want."

Kate smiled as she looked at her only granddaughter. Ellie was not just a grandchild; she was also a friend, a confidant, and at times, a partner in crime. They had been close since she was a baby. As a toddler just learning to talk, when anyone had asked Ellie her name, she always adamantly replied, "Elle," not Ellie. So, Kate tried to bow to the wishes of her granddaughter and switched between calling her Elle and Ellie. "No, Elle, I think I have everything together. I just need to throw all of it into a suitcase, and I'll be ready to leave this crazy place."

Ellie had just graduated from the University of Texas with a marketing degree. She had taken summer classes, in order to graduate in August. That would have been the perfect time for a summer cruise, but Ellie had wanted more time to settle back into normal life. Since her new job wouldn't start until mid-November, she wanted to celebrate right before the new job started. Kate suggested they take a two-week cruise in late October to the Panama Canal.

Years earlier, Kate had been through the canal while construction was going on for the new locks. Now that construction was complete, she was anxious to see what changes had been made. They were both looking forward to two weeks at sea, away from all the stress and strain of starting a new job and writing a long-anticipated book.

Kate had secretly hoped the relaxing vibes from an ocean cruise would overcome the lack of inspiration that had plagued her these last few weeks. She was also hoping that maybe the azure waters and gentle ocean breezes would tempt Edward to come back to her again.

When Kate first came up with the idea to write a book about the amorous adventures of a dashing pirate, she pictured a beautiful, black brigantine with the sails unfurled. A soft breeze gently guided the ship through the cerulean waters of the Caribbean. The ship was captained by an incredibly handsome but rugged pirate, who only plundered the Spanish galleons that were transporting confiscated natural resources of gold, silver, and precious jewels from the colonized islands back to Spain, where they would be used by the Spanish government. While Kate had no issue visualizing the setting and pirate, she had been unable to come up with a name or any details for her captain.

Personalization was an important mechanism Kate used in her previous books to establish a connection with the central character and help the story flow. Even after weeks, a defining identity for the pirate and a viable plot remained elusive.

As time passed, Kate grew increasingly frustrated with the slow progress of the story line. Frequently, she would sit at the computer, staring at a blank document file and silently cry out in desperation for the cosmos to please send a pirate from somewhere—anywhere—to help her. It appeared her supplications were unheard.

About four years ago, during a particularly violent spring thunderstorm with driving rain and strobe-like lightning, Kate slept soundly until a brilliant flash of lightning followed immediately by a loud clap of thunder jolted her awake. Still groggy from the depth of her slumber, she rubbed her eyes and looked towards the window. In the dim glow of the night light, she thought she caught a glimpse of movement but couldn't make out what was there. As her eyes adjusted to the darkness in the room, she could see a figure of a man standing by the window. She pushed herself up to a sitting position in the bed and quickly pulled the covers up to her neck as she stared warily at the apparition.

The man's good looks caught her right away. He stood tall and well-built, with long, wavy black hair and mesmerizing green eyes framed with thick, long eyelashes. Although he remained hidden in the shadows, Kate could see that he wore the typical clothing of pirates during the eighteenth century. He did not appear to be menacing, only confused as he stood there, rubbing his chin and looking around the room with narrowed eyes before catching sight of Kate.

As they cautiously eyed each other, thoughts raced through Kate's mind: Who was this person? Dressed as he was, could he be the answer to her many petitions to the universe? Was this the leading man she so desperately needed to help with the book? To ease her fears and help sort out the mystery, Kate rationalized that the gorgeous pirate in her room must be just a trick of her imagination—a phantasm that her mind was using to help move the novel forward. Readily accepting that conclusion, Kate relaxed and calmly asked her visitor who he was and why he was there.

"Madam, I be Edward Peregrine, captain of the brigantine the *Falcon*." His voice was soft, his tone uncertain. He took a cautious step into the room, glancing around at the furnishings visible in the dim light. "I dinnae know how I got here. I be readying the ship for an approaching storm when a white, hot light hit over me and knocked me to the deck. When I awoke, I be here. I dinnae want to scare ye." He continued scanning the room almost frantically, as though he was trying to find answers.

Kate smiled reassuringly. "I'm not scared. Actually, I have been asking for a pirate to come to me, and it seems you're finally here. I'm sure this is just a dream, and you are only a product of my subconscious, but this is very welcome inspiration."

Edward looked quizzically at Kate. "I dinnae know if ye be correct. I feel I be more human than just a dream. Where is this place?"

"You're at my home in Texas."

"And where be this Texas?"

"Oh, that's right. It wouldn't have been Texas during your time," Kate replied. "You are in North America."

"America? I be knowing of that land but never be sailing that far north."

Kate responded a little haughtily, "America isn't just a land. We are a developed, civilized twenty-first century country!"

"Twenty-first century? Milady, this be the year 1721. That hardly be the twenty-first century."

Kate's first instinct was to argue again, but she knew this was just a dream. Arguing with an eighteenth-century imaginary pirate hardly seemed worth it.

"Where are you from?" she asked instead.

"I be living on an island in the Caribbean."

"I should have known that I would end up with a pirate of the Caribbean after all those visits to Disneyworld with the kids."

"I dinnae know this place, Disneyworld, but I do be wondering why ye be thinking of having a pirate visit ye?"

Scooting more to the middle of the bed, Kate patted the side of the bed. "Why don't you have a seat while we chat?"

Edward walked over and hesitantly sat on the edge of the bed, then turned to look at her. A slow smile crept across his face. "Milady, if I may be so bold. I see that ye have a pleasing face and a winsome smile that puts a man at ease, but what is it that you want from a pirate?"

"I am a writer. My name is Kate Caldwell, and I write romance novels. I am starting a series of books with a colorful and very attractive pirate as the lead character. However, the plot is not coming easily to me. I have not been able to write a word. I have been making entreaties to the universe to send me a pirate to help with the book, and here you are."

Edward appeared uncomfortable with her explanation. He frowned and looked down then cleared his throat before responding. "I dinnae know how a book be written."

Seeing his consternation, Kate reached over and patted his hand. At the feeling of firm flesh and heat from his body, she pulled her hand away just as quickly as she'd reached out. It didn't seem possible someone who wasn't real could feel so tangible and human.

"I have the knowledge to write a book, but I need you to guide me and offer information from your experiences at sea. Together, we can come up with something that might reasonably happen to a pirate and develop a successful plot." Kate looked out the window. "I hope you will agree to work with me. Tonight, the storm is too loud for me to concentrate, but I trust you will return and enlighten me about life on the sea in the eighteenth century. You look the part of a seagoing man, and my book is about a handsome, dashing pirate and the women he meets."

Edward sat up and confidently replied. "Aye, then ye be having yerself a helper. I be knowing about the sea, the life of a pirate, and especially about beautiful young lasses, who might just take a fancy to me. I do believe I be the handsome type. What be the name of the book ye be writing?"

Kate thought a minute and then said, "I was thinking of *Passion on the Sea.*"

Edward laughed. "If the book be about passion, I be having the experience to help ye. I be visiting again, and we be writing a book." He winked at her and slowly faded away.

She lay in her bed going over the events of the night. Edward was a little brash in his character, but she had to admit, he was extremely good-looking. His Scottish brogue added another appealing touch. She could see where younger, inexperienced women might find him engaging and a little sexy, and he might be able to give her perspective on love during the 1700s. With that thought, she fell into a deep sleep.

The next morning, remembering the visitor during the night, Kate jumped out of bed, eager to get started on the book. She was happy she finally had a name and a face to put to her character. *At last, I can come up with a plot and get the book off to a good start.*

Her excitement turned out to be short-lived. The story was not as forthcoming as she initially hoped. She found herself anxiously waiting for another dream visit from her imaginary captain.

Edward did not disappoint. He made frequent appearances in her dreams as the weeks passed. Over time, the two successfully collaborated on the plots for the first two books in the *Passion* series. They worked together well and bounced ideas off one another, which led to some wild situations and very successful storylines.

Despite how easy it was to agree on the plots for the first two books, they quarreled over what Kate planned to be the final book. With the success of the beginning of the series, Kate wanted to end with the third book and promote the *Passion* stories as a trilogy. To give her fans a satisfying ending, Kate decided that this romantic adventure would introduce Edward to the girl of his dreams. The two of them would fall hopelessly in love, and Edward would leave the high seas adventurous life of a pirate to marry and settle down. Having learned of the story line, Edward vehemently disagreed with the plan. He was enraged about the direction Kate was leading his character. They argued back and forth, with Edward yelling that he was "too young to be put in dry dock" and that he'd "rather be keel-hauled than tied down to one woman."

"Another thing, Katie girl. Ye still be a single lady, so why do ye have a difficult time understanding why I have no interest in giving up the ways of a bachelor? Maybe I be settling down when ye decide to be a proper woman and get yerself a man!"

Kate rolled her eyes. "I'll have you know that I am a proper woman. These days, a woman doesn't feel she has to have a man to complete her. Women can do perfectly well on their own."

"Aye, but I be betting that in yer heart, ye sometimes wish for companionship and love. Ye just don't want to admit that these feelings are in ye. And while we be clearing the air," he added crossing his arms defiantly, "why do ye have me say *arrrgh* all the time? Real pirates never say *arrrgh*. The next thing I know, ye'll be havin' me with a peg leg, an eye patch, and a parrot on me shoulder! Just like the Disney pirates ye be telling me about."

Kate clenched her jaw, stewing in anger and ready to erupt. "Edward, you're thirty-eight years old. If you continue with your current lifestyle, you will become a caricature of a pirate. Besides, if you took the time to check a mirror, you might find that your flowing black hair is getting mixed with the gray strands of age, and your breeches fit a little tighter than in the previous books."

As soon as the words passed over her lips, Kate knew she had gone too far. There was a deafening silence between them before Edward turned to face her and icily replied, "Madam, ye have walked the plank. First, let me explain that there be no age in the reality ye have created for me. We all be equal;

however, I do possess feelings and desires. And ye, milady, have no understanding of what a man's needs be, in spite of the fact that ye evidently still stare at me pirate's breeches! Ye be so closed to life that ye now have the heart of a stone-cold dead mackerel!" With that, he turned and stormed.

Edward had not returned since.

His words stung, still ringing in her ears after days of silence from him. She wondered if there was any truth in what he said. Had she forgotten what love was like? Was she turning into a dead fish? Even if that was true, who did he think he was? Edward was nothing more than a figment of her imagination, and yet he placed himself in judgment of her. *Well, I'll show him. I can write this book on my own without his help.*

Despite her determination, after Edward's disappearance, Kate had been totally unable to develop the new storyline. Time ticked by, and her deadline for the new manuscript grew closer. She refused to believe that a dream argument between her and the character she created could possibly have resulted in her inability to get even one page written, but the facts spoke for themselves. As time passed, doubts began to chip away her resolve.

With the issue of her creative burnout, the clamoring public, and Sally's admonishment to spice up the sex—a statement that seemed to reinforce Edward's view of her as a cold fish who didn't understand men, though she still refused to admit there was any truth in it—the situation was making Kate more than a little anxious. She spent far too many days staring at the computer, watching the cursor taunt her with its incessant blinking as she stared at a blank page, unable to type a word.

It definitely was time to escape to a relaxing Caribbean cruise.

∽

Attempting to shake off the unpleasant thoughts from Edward's last visit, Kate decided it was time for a much-needed wine break before Ellie left for the mall. Lost in the memories of her journey with Edward so far, Kate had lost track of where she was and what she was doing. It was time to return to reality and prepare for her cruise.

As the two women walked down the hall towards the kitchen, Ellie tentatively asked, "So, has your captain been to see you lately?"

Kate couldn't help but smile. Ellie was more than a mini-Kate; she was her confidant and the only one Kate trusted to tell about the captain's nocturnal visits. Even as far-fetched as the idea was, Ellie had no problem acknowledging it as Kate's reality. Her acceptance of the dreams gave Kate the freedom to share the visits without fear of being thought a little dotty in the head.

The kitchen was Ellie's favorite room in the house. She always said that if Kate had not been a novelist, she could have easily become an interior designer. The large, inviting kitchen had the latest stainless-steel appliances complete with a double oven. While she had purchased them because she loved to bake for her grandkids, she could see the appeal of them in a contemporary home. After all, the white shaker cabinets and pewter hardware were a perfect match for the dark gray veined marble countertops. The fake sunflowers in the milk can on the counter served as the only pop of color in the room.

To lighten the mood after her depressing slant of thoughts with Edward, she said, "Alexa, play my favorite." Before Kate could uncork the bottle of Chardonnay she had retrieved from the wine cooler, the room was filled with the melodic strains of her favorite song, "Lonely Wine." As they listened to the soulful opening lyrics, she poured each of them a glass and answered Ellie's question.

"No, he disappeared right after the argument we had about him settling down and finding his true love. Like many men his age, he thinks he still has more wild oats to sow and should be good for another four or five books before we start deciding to put him in dry dock. He told me he would give up his freedom when I give up my single status and find a man to settle down with."

Kate swirled the wine in her glass, gazing at the movement. "Evidently, he also had been thinking along the same lines as Sally and had the gall to tell me there should be more explicit passion in the love scenes. I told him I just couldn't write things like that. I don't feel that all encounters between a couple have to turn into contortionist exhibitions. To me, there's nothing more sensual than understated passion. Imagine being with someone you care for and having him caress your face, fingertips barely touching your skin, while taking his time as he brushes a hand down your cheek to press his fingertips against your lips. That is so much more erotic than contrived moaning and forced heavy breathing."

Kate walked over and joined Ellie at the island, glass in hand.

"That does sound nice," Ellie said, "but so does a passionate night in the sheets. Maybe your editor and your captain know a little more than you think they do."

Kate didn't know whether to laugh or cringe at her granddaughter talking about sex, so she took a large sip of the rich, aromatic Chardonnay and shook her head.

Living so close to each other meant that Kate and Ellie spent countless hours together, sipping wine and enjoying each other's company. They always sat at the kitchen island and discussed anything and everything, solving the world's problems one bottle at a time.

When Ellie was younger, Kate would give her grape juice in a wine glass so Ellie could pretend she was a grown up. The two of them had spent many hours sitting on those bar stools solving teenage crises and boyfriend problems. Ellie could tell her grandmother things that her own mother might not want to hear. She knew there would be no judgment or criticism of her choices. There were times Kate would offer the benefit of her experiences and try to guide Ellie towards the right decision, but she made sure to allow Ellie the freedom to choose her own path.

"You know, Grandma, I overheard part of your discussion with Sally. Since you mentioned headboard-banging sex, I'm curious as to who you might consider sexy enough to be classified as a headboard-banger?" Ellie's eyes twinkled with mischief.

Kate laughed and shook her head, waving her hand at Ellie. "This is a ridiculous game, but since you asked, let me think for a minute about which men I might want to put into that category." Kate swirled the wine in her glass, then took a drink as she considered how much she wanted to divulge. "I usually don't judge that particular quality; however, I did go out with friends the other night to see a movie with Brad Pitt. I couldn't help but notice that since he's gotten a little age on him, he's looking pretty good. And then there's that sweet Matthew McConaughey. He's definitely a contender and always has been."

"Then why don't you use them as inspiration for the type of passion Sally keeps asking for?"

Kate rested her chin in her hand, lost in the mental images of men throughout her life that she'd been attracted to. She'd had many years to appreciate the male species and hoped to have more yet. Even so, there was a difference to the way she viewed men now. The days of wild abandonment were behind her, and frankly, she was glad. Her body just didn't bend like that anymore. She didn't think she even wanted it to. Lately, all she really longed for was connection. That was her struggle with what Sally and Edward both clearly thought to be an easy request.

She shrugged her shoulders and smiled. "As handsome as these men are, believe it or not, you reach a point in life where sex begins to take a backseat to basic human touch and comfort. I'm a leaner and have been all my life. Growing up, I always had my three older brothers to run to whenever I felt lonely or scared. I would grab their arm and lean up against them, knowing that nothing could harm me when they were around. Now that they're gone, I'm no longer a baby sister, and the comfort of having that kind of protection has been lost."

"What about Grandpa? Did you lean on him for protection?"

Kate looked away for a minute and sighed. "Yes, at first, he did give me that comfort. We used to sit on the couch and watch television. I would rest against his shoulder while holding his hand, and I had the same secure feeling I had as a child."

A cloud of sadness dimmed her spirits. It wasn't as if Robert had been a bad husband, but as time went by, he just couldn't give her the commitment she craved. "After your mother and uncle Joseph were born, there just didn't seem to be time for sitting together anymore. Or maybe we didn't make the time. I don't know. Whatever the cause, we began to drift apart. Your grandfather found other interests—and as you know, they were mostly female—and I began my career. Before long, we just lost each other. I promised myself that I would never marry again until I found someone who could give me that same feeling of reassurance and contentment I had known as a child and…well, we all know how that turned out."

The years after her divorce had only made her lonelier. Not that she didn't want the comfort of a man, but each one she met seemed more intimidated by her success than the last. Finding one who was simply interested in her as a person, and not what she could provide, had proved futile. Not one man in whom she had even the slightest interest proved to be anything beyond a disappointment. She shook her head to dispel the negative turn of her thoughts. She had plenty of blessings to be grateful for, and one of those blessings sat right beside her.

"You can still find love again, Grandma. It's never too late," Ellie said.

Kate laughed, though it felt hollow. "Oh, I think the days of whirlwind romance are over for me. But it's time to stop being maudlin. We have a cruise to look forward to! Let's get this show on the road so we can get an early start in the morning."

"Are you sure?" Ellie asked. "We can talk more, if you want."

Kate reached over and patted her granddaughter's knee. "No, that's okay. I think we ought to focus on better things ahead."

The conversation was over. Kate had packing to do and a book to write. Ellie kissed Kate goodbye and left for the mall, full of excitement for the next day. Kate knew that their candid discussion would be on Ellie's mind, but it was nothing she hadn't heard before. She trusted her granddaughter to follow her lead and put the past behind her.

Chapter Two

$\mathcal{T}$he drive from Kate's home outside of Austin to the cruise terminal in Galveston would take about four hours. They left early to ensure they had time for a late breakfast. Kate couldn't remember how the tradition started, but the two had never skipped the late morning meal on their numerous outings. This was their marker that signified they were officially on vacation.

After driving for two hours, they reached their favorite breakfast restaurant, Cracker Barrel, and eagerly headed inside for a much-needed cup of coffee served with a large country breakfast. They were practically dancing in their seats with anticipation of all the fun they would have in the next two weeks. Kate could hardly contain her optimistic hope that this cruise might inspire the last great novel to end her *Passion* trilogy.

As she ate breakfast, Ellie talked about all the food they had to look forward to on the ship. "Grandma, do you realize that we are going to have two weeks to eat whatever we want, whenever we want it?"

"Ellie, you are so funny. I really can't understand how you can be eating one thing and thinking about eating the next at the same time."

"I can't help it. The food on cruise ships is so good. With all the different options to choose from, you never have to grow tired of what you're eating. The best part is that we don't have to cook any of it! I think that's my favorite part about cruises."

"I like the solitude of the water and watching the waves break against the side of the ship. The view of the night sky is beautiful too. Without all the lights of a big city polluting the sky, you can see all the stars. You know me; I also love meeting new people and visiting new places. Your grandma's wandering spirit loves the newness of trips like this."

Ellie paused with her coffee cup in her hand and smiled. "This is going to be our best trip yet."

"I sure hope so." Kate smiled back and dipped her spoon in her grits for another bite. "But we will have plenty of time to enjoy everything over the next two weeks. For now, eat your breakfast and quit thinking about food."

Later, when they arrived in Galveston, Kate parked in one of the designated lots and they took the shuttle to the cruise terminal, where they left their heavy bags with one of the baggage handlers. They made their way inside the terminal to board the ship. After a lifetime of cruises, Kate always thought the boarding procedure took forever, but with this cruise, it went smoothly. Before she knew it, they were checked in and ready to explore.

The first area they saw was the atrium. As it would soon be Halloween, an imposing, fifteen-foot-tall pirate stood next to the stage. He wore a purple pirate frock coat with a stand-up collar and large gold buttons. He had black boots and green gloves, but instead of a head, he had a large jack-o'-lantern. An internal light made the eyes and mouth glow with an eerie green aura. He stood in front of a ship's wheel, with a looking glass in his hand and a green fish encircling his boots.

A line of eager passengers had already formed to have their picture taken with the oversized privateer. Large garlands of black, gold, and purple bows draped all the upper deck railings in the area.

"The decorations are so fun," Ellie said. "We should go on October cruises more often."

"You may not have the time when you start your big-girl marketing job."

"I'll always make time for you, Grandma."

Kate wrapped her arm around Ellie's shoulders and smiled. "How did I get so lucky with a granddaughter as sweet as you?"

After visiting all the public areas and getting the layout of the ship, it was time for a light lunch. They headed to the lido deck ready to indulge. Kate had a love for all things seafood, so when she saw bowls of shrimp, salmon, and other salads arranged in beds of ice, she was hooked.

When they finished their lunch, Kate and Ellie went to their suite to unpack and review the cruise's offered list of daily activities. Although they'd booked their shore excursions ahead of time, the daily activities on the ship were always a surprise until they arrived.

Their balcony suite had a small but comfortable sitting room and two bedrooms. This arrangement seemed to work best for them after Ellie reached her teen years and they both needed some privacy. The first thing Ellie did was check the mini fridge to make sure it was well-stocked. Even though she knew the snacks and drinks offered in their suite would cost a fortune, Ellie loved to let go and indulge on their trips. Kate enjoyed seeing her granddaughter relax and simply enjoy their trips, so she didn't mind.

"I cannot wait to swim with dolphins," Ellie said, cruise brochure still in hand. "It's always been something I've wanted to do. I can't believe we haven't been able to do that on any of our other cruises."

"It's always booked up by the time we book our shore excursions."

Ellie smiled sheepishly and shrugged her shoulders, setting down the brochure on the little side table. "Well, I guess we can be a couple of procrastinators sometimes."

Kate thought of the novel that had yet to be written, or even planned, and realized Ellie might have a point.

"You know, I'm excited to see—"

"Attention all passengers: please head to the deck and life-guard station listed on your boarding pass for a brief safety demonstration. We need all passengers to their assigned life-boat stations in fifteen minutes for a safety demonstration." The voice over the intercom echoed in Kate's ears, so loudly she could still feel the vibrations of the sound waves.

With so much cruise experience, they both knew this was coming, so they headed to their assigned deck as they were told and watched the safety demonstration.

After learning how to use a life preserver and where the designated lifeboat was located, they hurried upstairs to an open-air deck to watch the ship's evening departure from the Galveston dock. This was always one of Kate's favorite parts of a cruise. She loved getting to watch the shore grow smaller and further away. As the ocean grew larger, she felt all the worries and stresses of her routine life melt away into the waves.

This time was no different. Their excitement mounted at the deep throaty sound of the ship's horn and the view of the water churning from the force of the bow and stern thrusters separating the ship from the dock. Kate and Ellie gave each other a high five and then hugged. Their long awaited fourteen-day adventure had finally begun.

As the large vessel slowly left the dock and turned toward open waters, the two stood at the railing, watching the ship glide effortlessly through the calm channel towards the Gulf of Mexico. Even though it was late October, the southern sea breeze still felt warm on Kate's skin. The sun began to set, changing the low clouds to various shades of pink and orange. Other cruise ships followed in their wake out into the gulf on unknown adventures. Kate felt a deep sense of tranquility and appreciation at the beauty of the ocean's natural wonders.

Once they were far enough away that the details on the shore could no longer be seen, Kate glanced at her watch. "We better get ready for dinner if we're going to make our reservation."

"What do you think they're serving tonight?" Ellie slid her arm in Kate's as they headed down the stairs toward their room.

"I hope something good. I'm hungry." Her stomach rumbled in agreement. "The real question is, who will be our dinner companions?"

"Who knows? Maybe we'll be as surprised as last time. I still can't believe how funny Craig and Sharon were. They had the best stories from their shore excursions."

"I'm surprised they made it back alive after that excursion in Cozumel. Their story of the shady taxi driver and guy with a machete was wild."

"Remember that couple who only ever showed up the first night? I'm pretty sure they were newlyweds and spent the entire time in their suite, if you know what I mean."

Kate rolled her eyes. "You're terrible."

"No, I'm not. That's the kind of passion you need in your next book."

Kate thought of the couple, of the way they practically sat in each other's laps and spoon-fed each other bites of their meals. It seemed a little weird to her if she were being honest. She couldn't imagine incorporating that kind of "passion" in her novel. No way would Edward allow a woman to feed him his dinner.

When they arrived at their suite, each of them moved off to their separate rooms to change. Kate spent about fifteen minutes to get ready, while Ellie took a little more than twenty, before heading to the dining room.

"Look, some people are already here," Ellie said, pointing to their table.

Kate followed Ellie's gaze and saw four guests already seated at their table. There was a friendly looking couple seemingly in their early sixties sitting with a young man, who Kate assumed was their son. Next to the young man sat a handsome and distinguished looking gray-haired man.

He had the air of an academic, wearing a blazer with the classic elbow patches of a professor. His hair was cut just below his ears, a little longer than the standard length for a man his age. For Kate, the slightly longer hair was usually another indication of a professor. As she continued surveying their tablemates, the suspected professor in particular, she noticed he bore a strong resemblance to Edward. Her pulse quickened and her cheeks grew warm the closer they got to the table.

The waiter showing them to their table quickly pulled out their chairs and helped them settle in. Ellie smiled at everyone while Kate focused on unfolding her napkin on her lap.

"Welcome to the table," the man sitting with his wife said. "I'm Oscar Anderson. This good-looking blonde sitting next to me is my young bride, Amanda."

Amanda laughed and shook her head. "You're about thirty years too late with that compliment, dear."

"Better late than never," Oscar joked. He gestured to the younger man with them. "This is our son, Adam."

Kate looked over at Ellie, who had a bit of a blush in her own cheeks. She took over the introductions and said, "I'm Kate, and this is my granddaughter, Ellie."

"Pleasure to meet you both," Oscar said. "This is our first cruise. We're from San Angelo but have never made it this far south to try it out. Have y'all been on a cruise before?"

Kate smiled. "Oh, we've been on our fair share of cruises."

"Great! You two can give us the inside tips on how to make the most of it. We wanted to do something special since Adam here, our youngest, just graduated from A&M."

"Really? Ellie just graduated from UT."

Adam reached a hand across the table to Ellie. "Poor choice of school, but congratulations on making it through."

Ellie laughed and shook his hand. "I could say the same to you. Good thing you're finally out of that hell-hole."

The rivalry between A&M and UT ran deep, but it always amused Kate to hear students from each school make fun of the other.

"Do you have a job lined up yet?" Adam asked.

"Yes, I'll be working with the City of Austin in their public relations department. I'll be writing press releases and promotional material for various state magazines. You?"

"Adam is starting a new job when we get back from the cruise. He found an amazing opportunity with the Texas Railroad Commission in Austin," Oscar announced. Kate could tell from the beaming grin that he was proud of his son.

"Congratulations," Ellie said.

The man seated next to Adam spoke up, straightening his blazer as he introduced himself. "I'm David. I have to agree with Ellie here and apologize to Adam for his school. I'm an astronomy professor at the University of Texas."

"No!" Adam joked. "I need more allies here. We may have to switch tables."

David smiled. "All in good fun. I've been on a couple cruises before, but none this long. They're an excellent opportunity to get some good photographs of constellations. My goal this cruise is to capture the constellations in the southern Caribbean."

Kate smiled, satisfied that she had been spot-on with her assessment of him being in academia. She was also glad for the companionship of another fellow stargazer.

Just as David finished, a couple rushed over to the table,

practically knocking over their chairs in their haste to take their seats.

"So sorry we're late," the man said. "So, so sorry. Don't mean to interrupt. Please forgive our tardiness."

Kate couldn't help but notice that the man was tall and very attractive with salt and pepper gray hair and a beautiful smile. He introduced himself as Marco Antonini and the woman with him as his sister, Bettina. He seemed to look directly at Kate, making sure to hold her gaze, when he mentioned the word "sister."

"We've been on lots of cruises, but this one is special because it's a graduation present." Ellie's voice drew Kate's attention back to the table conversation. "Plus, my grandma's hoping to gather information for her next book."

"Oh!" Amanda practically jumped in her seat with her enthusiasm. "You're a writer? What books have you written? I read all the time and I might have read one of them."

Ellie sat up straighter and began explaining. "Her latest books have been about a pirate named Edward Peregrine, and—"

Amanda's fork clattered to her plate, the noise loud in the tall, open room. "Captain Edward Peregrine? You're Desiree Desire? I can't believe it! I've read all of your books, but the *Passion* series has become my favorite. You have made Captain Peregrine so completely handsome, charming, and gentlemanly, in spite of the fact that he's a pirate. He was so gallant in the first book when he saved that poor island woman from those hostile pirates who had pillaged her village. He seemed so gentle and caring with her. I think all my friends fell in love with him after reading that book."

Kate smiled and bowed her head quickly in thanks. "That's very sweet of you to say. Thank you."

"Desiree Desire! This is totally amazing. My friends will never believe me. We usually can't wait for the happily ever after at the end of romance novels, but with the *Passion* series, we just love seeing Captain Peregrine's adventures. He can settle down later! Everyone hopes you keep writing about him forever. I can't wait until the next book is out to see what kind of mischief he gets himself into this time."

"I can't wait to see what kind of mischief he gets into myself. This story line has proven to be a little challenging. I hope that being on the water will inspire me to place the captain in the middle of a very satisfying adventure."

"I'm a little curious about the appeal that a pirate holds as a leading character," David said. Kate was well-acquainted with the judgmental tone men had towards her books, but David didn't sound like them. He sounded genuinely curious, ever the academic. "From what Amanda said, I take it this fellow is a noble pirate, which in itself does seem to be an oxymoron. So, what is there about pirates so many women find attractive?"

Kate laughed. "I think it is the perceived 'bad boy' image they project. But the pirates in romance novels are not only handsome and manly, they are loving and dedicated to the happiness of their woman. If you think back, pirates have always been popular in romance novels and in movies. Who could ever forget Errol Flynn as *Captain Blood* or Johnny Depp and Orlando Bloom in *Pirates of the Caribbean*? There's just something very masculine and appealing about a hand-some, strong but gentle man who sails alone on the seas just waiting to find the one true love in his life. All I need to do is come up with a storyline that will help him find his love. That's the difficult part."

"Madam," Marco addressed Kate in a soft voice. "Any woman as beautiful as you should never have a problem writing about love. I'm sure your ideas will flow while relaxing on this wonderful journey."

Kate felt heat rushing to her face as she thanked Marco for his generous compliment. Ellie lightly kicked her under the table then hid behind the menu, laughing at how flustered Marco's comments made her grandmother. Fortunately, the waiter arrived to take their orders. No one else seemed to notice what had just happened.

"So, David," Ellie said, attempting to change the subject. Kate silently thanked her for the distraction. "I heard your intro to astronomy class was insanely difficult. I actually took geology for a science elective instead because of everything I'd heard."

"Oh, I like to think I'm not all that bad. I may be tough, but that's just because I expect a lot from my students. I set a high standard and help them meet it."

"Well, now that I've seen all the stars lit up on the view from the ship, I'm regretting not taking your class."

"I'd be happy to point out some of the constellations and various planets," he said. "Of course, there won't be any homework involved," he added with a laugh.

"How generous!" she joked.

"Actually," he continued, "another reason for the cruise is that I am on sabbatical this semester. I plan to do a feasibility study of offering a two-week course in celestial navigation for our upper-level students. Our school has access to a tall ship we could use as a classroom for a two-week course. Usually these are only for audit, but I hope to design it for credit hours."

"Wow! That sounds like a great class. I might have to go to grad school now," Ellie said.

"Ellie," Amanda asked. "What did you major in?"

"I have a marketing degree with a minor in journalism."

"From your description of your new job, it sounds like you also enjoy writing. Can we expect you to follow in your grandmother's footsteps and write a book someday?"

"That might be in the future, but I'll have to settle for mysteries or children's books since Grandma has cornered the market on romance."

Marco smiled at Kate. "There's always room for more romance in the world. With the genes you inherited from your lovely grandmother, I'm sure you would be equally successful."

Kate felt herself blushing again. She didn't expect to feel this way about someone the very first night of the cruise and debated internally over whether to give in or rebuff Marco's flirtations.

Isn't this what she hoped for, though? Marco could be exactly the inspiration she needed to find the plot of her last great love story for Edward.

Ellie took a sip of wine Kate hadn't noticed she ordered then asked Adam, "So, what's your degree in? I have no idea what you must have studied to work with the Texas Railroad Commission."

Adam laughed and nodded, like this was a response he was used to getting when sharing the news of his job. "I have an energy management degree."

"What prompted you to choose that as your major?"

"We have a ranch outside of Austin. It's been in our family for generations, but now the area around it is being taken over by companies looking for natural gas. It's destroying our land and the land of a lot of our neighbors and other farmers and ranchers in the area. I plan to monitor the environmental effects of fracking and drilling in the Permian Basin to hopefully protect our land."

David nodded, eyebrows furrowed as if deep in thought about the subject. "With young people like you taking up the stewardship of the state's land, we should be in pretty good shape."

Adam smiled. "Thanks, Professor Mitchell. I hope to make some kind of contribution. Our family ranch has been there since the 1800s. I want to make sure that our family, and all our fellow ranchers, are able to maintain operations for more generations to come."

Marco and Bettina had been a little quiet, but as the wine flowed with the food, Marco began to open up and share a little of their background. He told the group about life on the Amalfi coast, where they had lived until their parents died in an accident. After that, they were sent to live with their aunt in New York. Kate clung to every word, totally captivated by the story of their lives.

"Currently, I work in the shipping business, and Bettina is taking a break from her career. We came on this cruise so I could have a chance to see the Panama Canal and gain insight into the area. Many of my clients have offices in Cartagena, Colombia."

Kate's mind swirled with a thousand questions for Marco. Her own love of the Panama Canal dominated as she formulated questions about his work in the shipping business, but she found herself too reserved to ask them. She never felt shy, but something about Marco took the words from her mouth. She worried she might say the wrong thing, or ask a silly question, or seem too eager.

By the time dessert was served, the group had relaxed. They all agreed that their table was the best one in the dining room.

After dinner, everyone parted ways. Ellie pulled her grandmother aside and said that she wanted to go with Adam to one of the bars on the upper deck to listen to music and dance. Kate was glad Ellie was making a friend, and potentially more, with a young man who seemed so well put together for someone his age.

Kate briefly considered retiring to her room but found that she wasn't tired yet. It seemed silly to waste her first night on the cruise, but she felt at a loss of what to do.

As she considered the different places she could go on the ship, Marco said, "Ms. Caldwell, Bettina is a little tired and is going to her room. I'm not ready to turn in just yet and wondered if you would like to accompany me to the Salsa Bar for a nightcap and some wonderful music. I heard them playing while we were on the way to dinner. I think you might enjoy the entertainment."

"Mr. Antonini, that sounds like a wonderful idea. I'm still a little hyper from the busy day, and music always helps me gear down and relax. Just one thing though, you must call me Kate."

"Then we have a plan. If you are Kate, then I am Marco." Marco turned towards his sister and asked, "Bettina, are you all right to go to your room alone?"

Bettina smiled and nodded yes. "It was lovely meeting you, Kate. I look forward to our next dinner."

Marco held Kate's elbow protectively as he guided her through the crowded tables and made their way to the elevators.

The lounge on the promenade deck was busy. Marco glanced around and steered Kate towards a recently vacated table next to a window. A large bar took up the center of the lounge. From the size of the crowd, it seemed everyone on board was taking advantage of their first night at sea.

"I should go fetch us drinks. What will you have, Kate?" Marco asked.

"A frozen strawberry daiquiri," Kate answered. This was always her go-to when she wanted to relax and enjoy herself.

Marco smiled at her and winked. "Then a frozen strawberry daiquiri you shall have."

He disappeared to get their drinks, leaving Kate to hold their table. As she waited for his return, she found herself thinking of how nice it was to have someone get a drink for her. Rather than cut through the crowd herself, she could simply listen to music and wait to be served. Since she spent much of her life on her own, it was a good feeling to allow someone else to take care of her.

Just beyond the bar at the front of the lounge, there was a small group of musicians with a beautiful blonde singer fronting the combo. A small dance floor took up the space in front of the musician stage for anyone brave enough to try the fast, rhythmic, Latin dances. Marco had been correct— the music was excellent, and the drinks were good.

After a couple frozen strawberry daiquiris, Kate felt some of the stress of the day drain from her body. She was having a great time. Marco was entertaining and attentive. His stories of Italy were spiced with funny vignettes of growing up with many aunts and uncles, who always joined his parents for Sunday dinners until their passing. He only became a little less animated when he explained that Bettina was very ill, and the cruise was a way for her to get a lot of rest and hopefully recover some of her strength. The medicine she was taking precluded her from being in bright light, which limited her activities on the cruise. They would be staying on board the ship on port days so she would not be exposed to the rays of the brilliant Caribbean sun.

"I'm so sorry to hear that, Marco," Kate said. "It sounds incredibly difficult."

"We do the best with what we are given."

Kate resisted the urge to reach her hand across the table and touch him in comfort. She hadn't wanted to do that for a man in many years. The desire caught her off-guard.

The voice of the lounge singer broke through her thoughts. "Ladies and gentlemen, it's time for salsa lessons!"

Marco excitedly turned to Kate and took her hand. His touch was nice, and she regretted not reaching for him when the desire arose. "Let's go. We can't leave the ship without learning how to salsa."

"I'm not really good…" Kate tried to protest. She had loved to dance when she was younger, but nowadays, her Zumba lessons were the only practice she got. Marco took her hand and gently pulled her from her chair and toward the dance floor. With the help of the second daiquiri and the freedom from the stress that had gripped her for the past few weeks, Kate soon found herself on the black non-slip tiles with Marco and a few other brave souls trying to get the steps down as the singer gave out the instructions.

"Step forward with your right foot." The singer's encouraging voice commanded the amateur dancers through the steps, giving Kate a newfound confidence as she followed along. "Now bring the left foot up and quickly shift your weight back to the right foot. You can do this with a little twist of the hips. Now, step to the back and bring the other foot back and again shift your weight. Now, take a side step, and ladies, if you feel comfortable, take a little twirl while holding your partner's hand. Great! Now, all together, let's dance!"

The music started, and Kate felt as if she was being transported into a Fred Astaire/Ginger Rogers movie. She was surprised to see that she danced with grace, thanks in large part to Marco's expertise in gently leading and supporting her as she twirled into his arms. Kate found herself hoping the music would never stop. She had not danced in years. The excitement of the music's Latin beat, the effects of the alcohol, and the feeling of Marco's protective arms around her made her want this night to go on forever.

After the song ended, Marco led her by the hand to the quiet window table they had vacated. Luckily, it was still open and other patrons hadn't taken their seats.

Marco pulled out Kate's chair for her and pushed her in. She glanced through the window, admiring the way the light from the moon danced on the water below. Gazing at the moonlit water with its frothy white waves slapping against the side of the ship was something she had enjoyed on previous cruises. She was glad that this cruise was timed perfectly with the full harvest moon.

She turned to face Marco again, who had also been looking out the window. As their eyes met and held for a moment, Kate felt that the night couldn't be more perfect.

Marco reached for her hand again and laughingly said, "Hear that music? The band is back from their break. This night is made for dancing and losing ourselves in the rhythm of the samba."

"Marco, you are a glutton for punishment. I could totally destroy your toes dancing the samba," Kate teased. Now that they spent time dancing together, she was less shy about giving him a playful swat on the arm.

"My dear lady, I have no fear. Tonight, we are indestructible. We can conquer all dances and emerge victorious with all toes attached."

As the band played "Brazil," Kate accompanied Marco to the dance floor. Once again, they danced in unison and with grace, causing other dancers to stop to watch as they glided around the small dance floor in a perfect demonstration of how the samba should be danced. Kate felt truly free for the first time in years and allowed herself to let go, surrendering to the moment so that all else faded into the background. She didn't notice that she and Marco had suddenly become the center of attention, all eyes on them. The song barely ended when the band switched the beat and moved on to other dances.

They stayed on the floor, dancing and laughing until Kate felt the tiredness in her legs and knew that it was time for a break. As they turned together to walk back to the table, the band began the first few strains of a sultry tango. Marco looked askance at Kate as she playfully shook her head. She knew resisting was no use at this point. Marco was too good of a dance partner, and despite the soreness in her legs, she was invigorated by the fun of the night. She moved towards him, ready to take the first steps of what turned out to be a sexy rendition of the traditional South American dance of love. When the music ended, loud applause and whistles from the lounge patrons and a few passing passengers took her by surprise, forcing her out of the moment she'd created with Marco.

When they finally returned to the table, Kate collapsed in her chair, physically tired from all the dancing but relaxed from Marco's company. She was surprised at how quickly she began to feel comfortable with him. Because of her past, Kate had developed a guarded response to a man's attention. Her gut told her to turn around in fear, to resign herself to the true skeptic she thought herself to be, but Marco seemed different. She enjoyed how it made her feel to be looked at as a woman again; more than that, he appeared genuine. His compassionate personality made her feel safe, even after such a short amount of time with him.

Kate reached over and laid her hand on top of Marco's, unabashed and unafraid now. "Marco, I want you to know how very much I have enjoyed this evening. I've been so busy with work these past few months that I thought I had forgotten how to have fun. I appreciate being with you tonight."

Marco took her hand and interlaced his fingers through hers. "Kate, I feel the same. I hadn't realized how much I have been worrying about business and Bettina. Being with you tonight has shown me that I have been too locked away. After the death of my wife a few years ago, and now with Bettina's illness, I just withdrew from my personal life. I am so happy you are on this cruise and have shown me how to be alive again. In Italy, we have an expression: *Si canta sempre di cuore—quando si e pieni di vita.* This means 'One sings from the heart when one is full of life.' Tonight, I am overflowing with life."

She kept her hand in his for a moment as they sat quietly, looking out at the sea. Though she wanted to stay in this moment forever, she knew it had gotten late. She found herself fighting a yawn, despite how much fun she was having, so she rose from her chair. "It's almost midnight. I might turn into a pumpkin if I'm not in my room before the clock strikes."

Marco looked a little confused at her statement, but she whispered, "Cinderella." He smiled and nodded with understanding.

As Kate entered her room and closed the door, she kicked off her shoes and began singing, "I Could Have Danced All Night" while whirling around the room in her best Audrey Hepburn impersonation from *My Fair Lady.* After only a couple of turns, Ellie's door opened. "Grandma, where have you been?"

Kate stopped twirling and turned towards the bedroom door. Ellie stood there staring in wide-eyed disbelief at her grandmother, pajama clad arms crossed over her chest.

"Oh, sorry, Elle. I thought you would still be out with Adam. Guess you young folks just don't have it when it comes to partying."

Ellie raised her eyebrows and laughed. "Grandma, are you tipsy?"

"Yes, my dear. I'm tipsy on life. I've been drinking and dancing rumbas, sambas, and salsa like a pro." As an emphasis, Kate gave a little demonstration of each of the dances as she continued. "I had moves like Ginger Rogers with a little J-Lo thrown in for good measure. People were staring and clapping for Marco and me as we cleared the floor. It was freakin' fantastic! Marco was the perfect gentleman, and together, we made a phenomenal team. It was the best night I've had in many a year. I think I understand a little better now why Edward didn't want me to end his life of adventure. Fun and flirting are great for the soul!"

Having said that, Kate fell back onto the couch and began to giggle. She knew it was rare for Ellie to see her so fun and carefree. In all their time drinking wine and taking trips together, Kate couldn't remember the last time she'd let herself go like this. Laughing, she waved her bare feet at her granddaughter, a stark departure from her normally controlled, poised, and sophisticated self. The daiquiris must have relaxed her a little beyond tipsy.

Ellie took Kate's arm and pulled her off the couch. "Come on. Party's over. It's time to get to bed."

Kate could only smile. "I guess you're right. I am feeling a little tired."

They each headed to their separate rooms. Kate quickly changed out of her clothes and fell onto the welcoming bed. Almost as soon as her head hit the pillow, she was fast asleep.

⟿

"Kate, can ye hear me?" The deep, sultry voice seemed so far away.

Kate still felt stuck in her deep sleep, unsure if she really heard his voice again at last. "Edward? Is it really you?"

She forced her tired eyes open and sat up to look at the figure standing next to her bed. Seeing Edward again brought tears of happiness to her eyes. She did not realize how much she had missed him and how scared she had been that he wouldn't return. She stared at him, trying to etch his image into her memory in case he left her again. Edward got his muscles and strength from his Scottish father, but the shoulder-length black wavy hair and brilliant green eyes from his Irish mother. While he led the difficult life of a seaman, his eyes still shone with the tenderness of a loving and happy man. Kate could see why her fans loved him; he represented every woman's dream lover.

To Kate, he was her companion, her friend, and at times, her soul mate.

"Aye, Kate, 'tis me. Ye have the look of a happy woman. Does it have anything to do with the gentleman ye were dancing with tonight?"

"You know about Marco?" Kate asked incredulously. It always amazed her how Edward seemed to know everything that was going on in her life. She knew she shouldn't be surprised since he was a figment of her imagination, but she still thought of him as more of a friend.

Edward smiled, a twinkle of secret knowledge in his eyes. "I heard ye tell Ellie about your evening. It sounds like ye may have met someone who awakened in ye what ye had forgotten." He sat on the edge of her bed and gave her a playful nudge on the shoulder.

She smiled at the touch, but it quickly faded as she thought of the last time they spoke. "Edward, I'm so sorry about our disagreement. I really do understand why you want to continue with your exciting life as a pirate. I also had a chance to see how important you are to the fans of our books. I've been thinking that maybe I was a little too hasty in trying to turn you into someone who you are not ready to be."

"That be music to me ears, sweet lady, but there be some truth to what ye said. It might be time for me to have an adventure that would bring me to meet a woman who offers more than just physical appeal. Someone who wouldn't be just a conquest, but who would be a fine wench I might want to keep around for future adventures, if things go in that direction."

Kate nodded, glad to hear that Edward had seen some truth in her side of things too. She twisted a loose thread of the white comforter around her finger as she spoke. "Yes, Edward. I think you're right. However, if you keep referring to women as wenches, finding someone might be more difficult than I thought."

Edward stroked his five-day old beard that never seemed to get any longer. "Aye, Kate. Ye know what I mean. I would like a real lady, maybe even royalty. A woman who's intelligent, beautiful, possessed of an even temper—but also a woman who is passionate and adventurous."

"My goodness, Edward, you do have a lot of requirements. However, I really like the royalty angle. You're giving me some ideas. Keep talking, we might be on the verge of developing something."

Kate grabbed the notebook and pen she always kept by her bed for nighttime inspiration, ready to begin the collaboration she and Edward had worked out during the first two books. Their thought process seemed to work in unison. When one suggested a situation, the other would embellish it and take it to the next idea. Using that technique had always produced a viable storyline that would serve as a baseline for her book.

"Edward, what if you knew about a Spanish galleon taking gold back to Spain from the Caribbean islands? And on board, there was a Spanish duchess traveling with her handmaidens?"

"Aye, I could have a plan to steal the gold and kidnap the duchess to hold for ransom, but since she would be a comely lass, I would fall in love with her," Edward said, pacing as he talked. "And we would have a beautiful, passionate, and *sexual* relationship." At this, he turned to grin and waggle his eyebrows at her.

With the flood of ideas overpowering Kate's mind, she chose to ignore Edward's comment and focus on the story.

She blurted out her thoughts in rapid-fire excitement. "Okay, but we need to put in some elements to drive the plot. If you just kidnapped her and fell in love, the story would be over. There has to be something that would cause you concern about the kidnapping or the girl."

Edward continued pacing, deep in thought. In the blink of an eye, he froze in place and turned towards her, throwing his hands into the air as a thought struck him. "What if I know that there be another ship after the galleon, and they have bad intentions towards the duchess? My ship could reach the galleon first, quickly take the treasure and the girl to protect her from merciless pirates that roam the sea."

Kate mulled it over, nodding as she scribbled the thought down. "I like that. What if you don't know which girl is the duchess, since the true duchess had changed into her maid's clothes to protect her identity? The whole voyage back to England would be written around you trying to discern which captive is the real duchess."

"That be a good idea. And while we be sailing, I could find that I fancy one girl especially—perhaps a lass with red hair—but not be sure whether she is the real duchess or the handmaiden. She would return me favors, of course. We'd be having many exciting romantic moments together, which ye would write about in minute detail." He raised his eyebrows again as he stared pointedly at her for the last sentence.

Kate was already aware of the expectations for this book, and the repeated reminders began to irk her. She huffed and spoke a little sharply. "Edward, you have a one-track mind. You've mentioned lovemaking more than once tonight. I promise to work on the romance parts, but not every scene will involve sex." She looked out the balcony door, taking deep breaths to calm herself down before she spoke too soon and caused Edward to leave again. "We need something more to make the plot pop, possibly a big event, something that would be scary and cause the girl to reveal her true identity. Something that could threaten the ship and make her fear that they are going to die. What could happen on a ship at sea?"

"Aye, that be easy. Every day at sea is a potential for disaster. What if we be hit by a sudden storm with high winds and buffeting waves? The helmsman could injure his arm trying to hold the wheel in full wind while the men put up the storm jib. In an act of sheer bravery, I rush out in the midst of the storm to steer the ship into the waves to keep it from rolling over. Me love, fearing for me safety and willing to sacrifice her own life, comes running to help."

"That is just what we need. Maybe a violent storm like the one we had the night you first came to visit me?"

"Aye, that be a tremendous storm. The wind and rain pounded the waters with a vile force, but it be the lightning that produced the most fear. In all me years at sea, never have I seen such an electrical storm as that. There be a feel of the powerfully charged air with the jagged bolts never seeming to stop even for a second. It was as though the massive electrical energy of all time had opened and closed back on itself." Edward paused and closed his eyes, shuddering at the memory of the storm he had witnessed. "I hope to never see a storm like that again in me life. For our story, I think we just be having a regular storm at sea."

"I agree. Just a normal, everyday type of thunderstorm with normal lightning." Kate imagined what would take place. She saw it all play out like a movie in her head: Edward bursting out into the rain, shouting to be heard over the winds; his love daring to brave the storm and leave safety to help him, clinging to him as the ship rocked back and forth.

Kate smiled at Edward and tried to give voice to the vivid image in her mind. "Edward, it would be so romantic. Just imagine, you and your love lashed together at the wheel, struggling side by side to keep the massive ship pointed into the waves through the storm. All the while, rain is beating against your bodies with lightning striking the water nearby. The woman stays brave and strong in her desire to stand side by side with her true love."

"And since she be so much in love with me, she confesses that she be the handmaiden. If she is to die, she not be wanting to die with a lie on her lips."

"Then you declare you love her with the burning love of desire."

Edward tilted his head, then shook it, seeming to be lost in thought. "It need be something more powerful. Maybe I love her with the burning passion of the sun."

"I like that, but what about the passion of the burning sun?"

"If ye do the job properly and write the lovemaking the way it should be, it has to be more than the passion of only one sun. It be the fiery passion of a thousand burning suns."

As soon as the words passed Edward's lips, Kate knew in her heart it was perfect. "That's it!" she shouted. "That's the name of the book: *The Fiery Passion of a Thousand*

Burning Suns! This is our book. My inspiration is back. I can write again! Let me get started and later we can work out more details of the story and what will happen to the real duchess."

Brimming with excitement, Kate leaned over and tightly hugged Edward where he stood next to her bed, thanking him profusely for helping her again.

"Aye, Kate. Ye be spilling over with ideas that be coming faster than an overtaking sea." Edward paused, looked down, and shifted his weight before adding in a soft voice, "Ye also will be remembering about adding a little excitement to the romantic encounters? If ye do, I just want ye to know that I be in agreement with anything ye might think of to add the spice Sally wants." As he spoke, he seemed to get a little fainter in her dream. "Kate, this be a good visit. I feel that the next time ye touch the computer, words will flow from ye like the strong currents of a troubled sea."

After the excitement of having ideas, thoughts, and story lines filling her brain, Kate was ready to drift back into a deep, dreamless sleep. As the welcome slumber engulfed her, she thought she felt the warmth of Edward's breath and the gentleness of his fingertips softly touch her lips as he leaned down to whisper, "Sleep for now, Katie girl. But remember, someday belongs to us."

Hearing his parting words, she was unsure whether he had really spoken or whether she had dreamed them. While she had no idea what he meant by *someday belongs to us,* she couldn't help but think it was important and something she shouldn't forget.

Kate woke early the next morning and jumped out of bed. She smiled, letting the relief of her reconciliation with Edward wash over her. As she recounted their conversation, excitement stirred in her chest as she remembered all the ideas rolling around in her mind. She called room service for breakfast and then took the quickest shower of her life, eager to get started writing. Ellie had already left to meet Adam for an exercise class based on the note she left on the coffee table in the sitting room, which left Kate plenty of time to work. After showering, she threw on casual linen cropped pants and a navy-blue crewneck tee. She finished dressing just as her breakfast arrived.

The room service attendant placed the tray on the balcony table while she gathered her laptop and notes. Kate always loved having her breakfast on the balcony when she traveled. The open view of the waters and the gentle sway of the ship may have turned others green with seasickness, but to Kate, they calmed her nerves and gave her a feeling of peace and relaxation. As she looked out over the waves, bright from the dancing reflection of the sun, she could see another ship off in the distance. Seeing the small size of the other vessel made her realize just how large the ocean was and how alone they were in their own little section of the water. The isolation had a calming effect on her, much like the view of the open water that balanced the hectic pace of life.

After a delicious croissant and fresh fruit, she took a sip of coffee then set down the cup on the desk, ready to get started. This was the moment of truth. Had Edward been right? Would the words come flowing from her mind as he had said?

She opened her laptop and put her fingers to the keys. The time of reckoning was here.

Chapter Three

THE FIERY PASSION OF A THOUSAND BURNING SUNS

Millie

The three women huddled together, a mixture of fear and excitement in the air as they clung to each other. They could see the sleek black brigantine, with sails trimmed for speed, rapidly approaching their heavily ladened galleon.

In fear for their lives, Millie cried out, "Oh milady, what are we to do? The ship is getting closer."

The women had been instructed to go below to their mid-deck cabin while the beautiful galleon, the Santa Magdalena, *tried in vain to outrun the pirate ship. Not sure of the gravity of the situation, all three young ladies crowded around the narrow porthole, trying desperately to view what was happening. One of the women was Lady Teresa del Gado, niece of the Grand Duke and Duchess of Seville.*

Lady del Gado had traveled to the Caribbean Islands to visit her older brother, Jorge, who was in service there with the government in Cartagena. The other two women were her maidservants and had been with her for several years. Millicent, or Millie, was the older one and was blessed with the same beautiful red hair and clear green eyes that Lady Teresa possessed. It was often said that they were similar enough to be sisters. Sophia was the youngest and attractive in her own right, with thick black hair and piercing brown eyes. Upon her sixteenth birthday, she had been placed in Lady Teresa's service and enjoyed her duties and position immensely. All three had formed a fast friendship and were known to laugh and tease more like equals rather than royalty and commoners.

Since Millie was the older maidservant, she took the responsibility of looking through the porthole and reporting what she saw. Lady Teresa's safety depended on her.

"Lady Teresa," Millie said, looking through the porthole again, "I can see the black color of the ship. It looks like it is flying the flag of the Falcon." She lifted a hand, pointing at something behind the brigantine. "But there is another ship in the distance, farther back from the first ship, and it looks like it is chasing us too."

The pirate ship, the Falcon, was well known in the Caribbean along with its captain, Edward Peregrine. Captain Peregrine and his men were notorious for commandeering ships, occasionally kidnapping travelers—mostly female—but only taking half of whatever treasure the captured vessel carried. The kidnapped victims were always returned to their homes, even though some of the women seemed more inclined to want to stay with the ship and its captain. Upon completing its looting and piracy, the ship would hurriedly sail off and disappear into the vastness of the sea, unable to be found.

Authorities had been half-heartedly looking for him for years, but since the captain was not violent and was not known to have ever harmed anyone, they didn't put too much of a priority on the search. There were far worse men to pursue.

The Falcon *had been known to keep other pirates away from the Spanish galleons, which meant less of a loss for the Spanish government. Once the more barbaric pirates saw the heavily armed* Falcon *had claimed a ship, they retreated from the area to look for other prey. The islanders had no interest in having the* Falcon *caught, since its captain had always given the largest portion of his pilfered treasure to share with the impoverished peoples of the Caribbean.*

"I think it is Captain Edward Peregrine!" Millie exclaimed. "He is rumored to be the most handsome pirate on the sea. There are tales from the women he captured about his expertise in love. He is unparalleled."

"Millicent! That is enough," admonished Lady Teresa. "Can't you see that Sophia is afraid?"

Millie sighed and wrapped her arm around Sophia. "Don't worry, Sophia. He will only be interested in Lady Teresa, since she is royalty and could bring about a rather large ransom."

"Interested in me?" Lady Teresa scoffed at the accusation. "I would never have any man who serves on a pirate ship take advantage of me. My uncle would never stand for it. Captain Peregrine would be shot if he tried."

"Lady Teresa, your uncle is not aboard this ship, and as such, he would not be able to do anything until after the fact," Millie reminded her. "We need to devise a plan to protect you and keep Captain Peregrine from knowing which of us is the real Lady Teresa del Gado."

Thanks to their similar looks, Millie immediately had a plan in mind. The other girls followed her lead and busily disguised Lady Teresa by dressing her in some of Millie's clothing. They stuffed Lady Teresa's dress through the porthole and into the sea. This took a lot of finesse given the layers of fabric and skirts, but Millie hoped the captain would see the royal dress floating in the water and think the poor girl had drowned at sea rather than be kidnapped by a ruthless pirate.

They unpinned Lady Teresa's hair and let the flowing copper-colored curls cascade down below her shoulders. Lady Teresa removed all her jewelry and put it in a hidden box under her bed. Having finished the dressing, the girls fitted silken snoods over their hair and surveyed their work in the small, cloudy mirror in the cabin.

Millie nodded, satisfied with her plan. "This will work. Captain Peregrine will never be able to spot the real Lady Teresa."

"Perhaps his inability to determine the true royalty will cause him to give up and let all three of us go," Sophia added, still uneasy but clearly less fearful than she was only minutes ago.

After a valiant run, a shot over the bow of the galleon eventually brought the race to a finish. The brigantine pulled alongside the galleon. Millie watched through the porthole as grappling hooks attached to ropes pulled the two boats together, making it possible for Captain Peregrine, a man who looked to be his navigator, known as Henry Armitage, and some of the captain's men to board the defeated ship. The three port side cannons on the brigantine were aimed directly at the galleon ready to fire, probably a precaution against any resistance on their part. Millie knew that should anything threaten the captain or his navigator, there would be no escape. The starboard side cannons were pointed in the direction of the other advancing ship, which now seemed to be making a turn away from the galleon.

As the ship was boarded, the three women ran to the stairs and tried to get a look at what was happening. Millie was the first to spot the captain. She almost squealed out loud when she caught her first glimpse of the famous pirate. He jumped onto the deck, close to the stairs where the girls were hiding. "Oh milady," she whispered. "He is the most handsome man I have ever seen."

The other two moved closer to where Millie stood, trying to capture her view of the deck.

"He is so tall," exclaimed Sophia, "and he has the most beautifully wild black hair. I can see how the curls frame his face and magnify his eyes."

"I've heard they're the most vibrant green you've ever seen," Millie added.

Lady Teresa spoke up, reprimanding them in a harsh tone. "Sophia. Millie. Remember he is a pirate, intent on doing us harm—"

Before she could finish, Millie sighed. Lady Teresa always was the level-headed one, but Millie couldn't help herself as she gazed upon Captain Peregrine. In a soft, breathless voice, she said, "He is so strong. Look at the way his shirt fits tightly across his chest, barely able to contain the muscles within. I do not see an extra ounce of fat on his body. And his breeches seem to cover sturdy legs, poised for a fight. He'd be ready for danger at a moment's notice, or perhaps even be ready for love."

"Girls!" shouted Lady Teresa before she caught herself. The ladies exchanged glances, each of them wide-eyed and silent. But they knew it was too late. Captain Peregrine had heard them.

Edward

At the sound of the women's voices, Captain Peregrine turned and caught just a glimpse of the retreating females heading back to their cabin. Having received a dispatch from the Grand Duke of Seville, informing him of the traveling arrangements of his niece and her handmaidens, Edward knew in advance that the women would be on board. The grand duke was an acquaintance of Edward's brother and hoped that Edward would give thought to protecting Lady Teresa from other privateers on her voyage. He turned to his navigator and suggested they head downstairs to pay a call on Lady Teresa del Gado.

Edward pushed open the door to their cabin, looking at the three women. "Greetings to ye, me fair maidens. To whom do I have the pleasure of meeting?"

The girls stood silently and made no sound.

"Ladies, did ye not hear what I just asked?"

One of the girls finally answered, an air of confidence in her voice. "Oh Captain, it's so horrible. Lady del Gado flung herself into the sea during the chase, saying she would rather die than be subjected to a fate more horrible than death." As she spoke, the girl softly dabbed her eyes with a handkerchief, soaking up what Edward knew were likely fake tears of despair.

The girl's theatrics were some of the best he'd seen, but it didn't deter him. Rather, her statement that he would be worse than death irritated him. He knew his reputation to be good and fair, so why did women still insist on acting this way? "So, death is preferable to me? Is that what ye be trying to tell me?"

"Oh Captain, it is not what we think. It is what Lady Teresa thought. I do not think that you are that bad a person," the same girl said. The girl standing in the middle nodded her head in agreement.

"Not that bad? Well, I think ye might have meant for something in what ye said to make me feel better, but ye did not succeed. I dinnae believe ye anyway. I think one of ye be the lady, and we are going to find out which one."

As the Captain approached the three girls, they fearfully stepped back in unison. They moved as far away from the captain as possible in the small cabin. He grunted in frustration at their persistent fear. One way or another, Edward was determined to discover the true identity of Lady Teresa.

"All right. First, we need to see your hair. I know that Lady Teresa del Gado has beautiful hair the color of the setting sun as it falls beneath the waters of the ocean."

As he stepped in front of Sophia, he gently untied the hair covering, releasing long, black hair that fell gently to her shoulders. She looked at the captain with dread in her thickly lashed brown eyes. She shivered where she stood and seemed afraid he might do her harm.

Exasperated, Edward nearly shouted at her, "Girl, why do ye look at me in anguish? I know ye not be the lady. Ye shall be free to sail back to Spain with the ship. I do want ye to deliver a dispatch to the grand duke telling him that we be docking in Portsmouth in about sixty days to return Lady del Gado and the other young lass." Saying that, he walked over to the desk and quickly wrote the message Sophia was to deliver.

After dismissing the raven-haired girl, Edward signaled for another girl to step forward. He repeated the same steps of removing the hair covering and allowing the hair to fall smoothly out of its confinement. This time, the hair was red. How simple that was, Edward thought as he ran his fingers through the luxurious strands of copper.

"Aye, ye must be Lady Teresa del Gado, as ye have the hair she is known for. This has been an easy task." Satisfied he had discovered the truth, Edward waved his hand in dismissal towards the girls, bragging about his superior ability to solve any riddle.

As he spoke, the girl whose hair he had not yet uncovered took a step forward. Determination in her eyes and jaw clenched tightly, she loosened her hair covering to reveal similar beautiful flowing red hair. Edward looked from one girl to the other. They had the same hair and eye color. This girl had been the one taking the lead in speaking with him, but that could mean anything. Either she was the real Lady Teresa del Gado, leading as was her right as royalty, or she was the lady's maidservant, protecting the grand duke's niece at all cost.

"Ye have produced a dilemma," Edward pronounced. "It is best if I take each of ye to another cabin and try to determine the truth."

As he spoke, Edward walked over to the defiant girl. "Ye be the first to come with me. We will soon learn who ye really be."

⚬◠⚬

Millie

Millie thought she might have been more frightened if Edward had not been so handsome. She'd always been told she was a strong-minded and worldly girl, and in this moment, she found that to be true. She was more challenged by Edward than afraid.

Aye captain, she thought, we'll be playing your game, but I warn you that you might find me a formidable opponent.

As Millie and Captain Peregrine entered the adjoining cabin, she turned to face him, waiting to see what might happen. Her first impulse was to kick him in the shins, but that would not be the act of a lady. He would know immediately she was not the one he sought.

Edward stood directly in front of her, looking her up and down. Appreciation shone in those exquisite green eyes he was famous for. He examined every detail of her face and body while Millie stood frozen in place. She hated to admit it, but she was excited to be so close to a man with such a famed reputation. His appreciative gaze made her feel warm.

He whistled as his eyes dragged their way up her body. "Ye be a beautiful woman. I have heard tell of the beauty of Lady Teresa del Gado. Ye could fit that description, but I think ye need to be truthful with me and admit your identity."

Never one to remain silent, Millie replied, "Captain, I have nothing to say." She knew Lady Teresa would be too demure to speak so defiantly, but Edward seemed only familiar with her looks and not her temperament. Millie had known many royal women to be so bold so her natural stubbornness wouldn't give her away.

"Aye, so ye be wanting me to find out for me self, is that it?"

Edward smirked, eyes still roaming over her body. He seemed to think he had a fool proof plan to discover their identities.

But Edward didn't know that the women anticipated the method he might use to discover the real Lady Teresa. His romantic dalliances were well-noted among everyone Millie knew, and it seemed obvious he would use his charm to gauge how each woman would react. According to royal expectations, Millie would act the proper virgin, while Lady del Gado would be flirtatious and responsive to the captain in an effort to confuse him.

Millie caught her breath as Edward ran his fingers through her hair down to her neck. With a slow glide of his fingers, he lightly brushed them up to her ear where he circled the outer edges, teasing the skin with a featherlight touch. She stood as still as she possibly could, trying not to give herself away by reacting to his touch, though she could feel heat rise in her cheeks.

Millie stared directly into those forest green eyes and said, "I know I cannot overpower you, so I must be ready to accept whatever it is that you do to me. But I can promise you that I will not enjoy even one second of having you close to me."

Her voice came out huskier than she intended. The power he was weaving threatened to break her resolve. She struggled to hide the flush of her skin, the fire in her eyes, and the heat from her body. Her response belied her words. With delight, she noticed that his own response was equal to hers. There was a fire in his breeches just from the closeness of their bodies.

She composed herself enough to say, "Do with me what you want, but I shan't tell you anything. If you force yourself on me, I will fling myself into the sea at first chance." Her voice turned to a whisper as he drew closer until their bodies touched.

She felt the rise and fall of her breasts against his chest. Her breathing grew heavier. He traced a finger down her throat to the rise of her bosom and moved lower to touch the hardness of her...

◯

*K*ate heard the door of the suite open as Ellie returned from her morning adventures.

"Grandma?" she called. "How's the writing going?"

Kate smiled at her granddaughter, relieved to finally have made progress with the book. "Better than I could have hoped. The words are simply flying from my fingers."

"Great, then let's go get some lunch. I'm starving. I think they're having a seafood extravaganza on the lido deck."

"Sounds wonderful. Let me save my work, and I will be ready."

"Kate!" Edward shouted. "What ye be doing? Ye cannae stop writing now. Keep typing. His fingertips moved lower to touch the hardness of her what? What is he touching? We be in the middle of a delicate situation here, one that requires ye continue to write the words. I beg of ye, please dinnae press *Save*. Continue writing! Dinnae leave me be in this particular position. DEAR GOD, WOMAN WRITE THE BLOODY WORD!"

With a sardonic smile, Kate firmly clicked the save button, ensuring her work wouldn't be lost, then saved it again to her thumb drive before closing the computer and taking it to the desk in her room to recharge.

"Something very strange happened when I closed the laptop," she said to Ellie, who sat on the small chair in the shared room, ready to go. "I distinctly heard someone say *arrgghhh*."

"You mean *arrgghhh* like a Disney pirate?" Ellie laughed.

"Well yes. Exactly like a Disney pirate." Kate laughed and shook her head. "I just realized that I am hungry. I believe I could eat a stone-cold dead mackerel. Let's go."

Chapter Four

The day passed quickly. Kate became so engrossed in her adventures on deck that she almost missed dinner. Ellie found her relaxing in a lounge chair by the pool and reminded her that dinner would start in thirty minutes.

By the time Kate and Ellie arrived at the table, their friends were already seated, sharing stories of their first full day at sea. Kate couldn't help the flutter in her heart as she spied Marco sitting at the table with his sister. And as luck would have it, the seat next to Marco remained open.

Kate took the open chair and smiled at Marco as she sat down. He grinned back at her, the two sharing a secret look before turning their attention back to the table.

Adam was just starting to tell everyone about his day with Ellie. "We started with a good work out in the fitness center, then met up later at the pool."

"Adam had no idea there were so many activities by the pool. He thought people just went there to swim." Ellie laughed.

"What else would someone do at the pool? Apparently a lot. There was even a hairy chest contest."

"I still think you should have joined. Just for fun," Ellie teased.

He shook his head. "Never in my life."

Kate smiled as she watched the two tell the story of their day together. Even after such a short amount of time, they seemed to have really hit it off. Since Kate had a front row seat to Ellie's misadventures in dating, it was nice to see her with someone so compatible.

As if they knew her thoughts, both of them started laughing at the same time and pointing at each other.

"Oh my gosh, remember that woman who definitely spent way too much time at the swim-up bar?" Ellie asked.

"Only alcohol could convince a woman to try and take part in a hairy chest contest."

"Well, it's discriminatory!" Ellie laughed, shook her head, and wiped tears from her eyes.

Oscar and Amanda smiled at the young couple. Kate could tell they were equally happy to see them getting along so well.

"So how did they resolve it?" Oscar asked. "Did she join the contest?"

"The assistant cruise director, Casey, wasn't sure how to respond. You could tell she was so startled at the idea that the woman might actually remove her top to display her un-hairy chest," Ellie answered.

Adam continued, "Everyone who had gathered around to watch the contest just stared at the woman, wondering what would happen next. Then the lady shouted, 'Just kidding, Casey. Wanted to spice up the contest a bit!'"

"The crowd laughed and clapped as she left the stage and went back to her lounge chair. You could see Casey just kind of collapse with relief as she left," Ellie finished.

Kate listened as the others recounted their days. Oscar and Amanda had a little less provocative day. They played trivia, then joined another couple for a round of bridge. David mentioned he spent time in the library reading and, by his own admission, dozing in a comfortable leather lounge chair. Marco and Bettina enjoyed shopping and spending time in the casino.

When Kate revealed that she spent a good portion of her day writing, everyone at the table was interested in knowing what the story was about. Amanda, in particular, was curious about the women who would capture the captain's fancy. Kate hesitated to give out too much information, carefully speaking of her story in vague terms. She knew from experience that as a story line developed and the characters began to form their own personalities, plot twists could take the book in a different direction. Aside from that, she'd been admonished by Sally for giving her readers a little too much information before the book was released.

"Don't ruin the suspense," Sally always told her. "Your readers aren't going to buy the book if you tell them everything before it's released. No sales, no job!"

By the time dessert was served and everyone took their last indulgent bites, music began playing. All the food servers started singing and dancing as the guests watched with delight and filmed it on their phones. There was a lot of napkin waving and clapping from the servers to encourage the whole dining room to take part in the song. A few brave guests started a conga line that wound its way through the tables like a giant caterpillar on a tomato plant.

Soon, it was time to go, and the group began heading out for their individual activities. Kate stood, taking her time replacing her napkin on the table and pushing the chair in just so.

Marco caught on to her dawdling and stepped close to her side. "Kate, I was wondering if you would like to join me again for a drink and more dancing."

Usually quiet, Bettina smiled and nodded, while moving her hands in a brushing motion to encourage Kate to go. "You really should. I'll be fine in the room. Marco so enjoyed his evening last night, and I want you two to have another fun time."

With Bettina's blessing, Kate nodded. "It would be my honor. Thank you for your blessing, Bettina."

"Well then," Marco said as he took Kate's arm. "Let's go shake up the dance floor."

"Tonight, I wore more comfortable shoes, so I'm ready for whatever the music offers." She looked up at Marco and laughingly added, "Let's go show the young people how seniors really live."

The lounge was a little more crowded than it had been the night before. Luckily, Marco and Kate again found an empty table beside a window. It was as if fate wanted them to have a quiet table together. By the time they were seated, a waiter appeared to take their drink order.

"I think I'll try a frozen margarita tonight." Kate didn't usually order margaritas, but tonight felt like a night for trying new things.

"That sounds good. Make it two." Marco moved his chair closer to hers. She knew it was probably so they could hear each other better, but Kate hoped he also just wanted to be near her. "So, your day went well and your book has begun?"

"Yes. I had a very productive day. It feels so good to be writing again. I'm not used to having lengthy difficulties with story lines, but there just seemed to be a lot of pressure getting this book going."

"You must be very good at what you do to have so many bestsellers."

"I have been lucky. The latest series has turned out to be the most popular. Women seem to really enjoy the adventures of my seagoing pirate, despite his raffish ways. I guess women really do like the bad boy image." Kate laughed, amused by the way some clichés seemed to be a cliché for a reason.

Wanting to focus back on Marco, she asked, "How is Bettina feeling? Is the ocean air helping her?"

His smile faded and a sad look came over his face. "Bettina had cancer and was in remission for almost three years, but we found out last month that it has returned. The doctor suggested we take this cruise to give her a little fun before she begins a difficult and expensive experimental chemotherapy. She has been on the waiting list for this new drug for about six months. We just got the notification that her treatment will begin next month."

"Marco, I'm so sorry. I didn't realize she had such a difficult illness." After their time together last night, Kate no longer felt shy about touching Marco. She reached a hand across the table and placed it over his in comfort.

"It's all right; you couldn't have known. I've tried to stay positive for her, but secretly, I've been worried about the treatment. She doesn't have the best health care insurance, and with the slowdown in my business, I'm worried about the physical and financial aspects of her illness. Hopefully, the trip to Cartagena will help me secure an investor who has shown an interest in my company. If this meeting goes well, we can finalize the deal; in a short time, we will be back on top again. If the deal doesn't go through, well…" Marco stopped and took a sip of his drink before turning his hand over, pressing their palms together and wrapping his fingers around her hand. "Enough of sad subjects and what ifs. Tonight is for happiness and dancing."

He kept Kate's hand in his while he stood, pulling her with him as he headed towards the dance floor. Just as she did last night, Kate had no difficulty following his expert guidance. Their movements were perfectly in sync, as if they'd been dancing together for years. An admiring crowd soon gathered to watch them again. When they returned to their seats, an attractive young lady followed them to their table. Kate recognized her as the assistant cruise director Adam and Ellie were talking about earlier, Casey Phillips. Casey sat down in an empty chair she pulled over from an adjoining table.

"Hi! I'm Casey, one of your cruise director's fearless helpers. I've noticed the two of you dancing for the past couple of nights, and I wanted to invite you to be in our passenger dance contest that will be held the last formal night of the cruise."

Kate couldn't help but laugh. The thought of her competing in a dance contest at her age seemed ludicrous. "You want us to compete with all the young talent that is on this ship?"

"Hey, I've watched you two, and I really think you could walk away with the winning prize. By the way, it's a free seven-night cruise out of Galveston to a Caribbean port of your choice. It would give you a chance to show just how 'with it' seniors can be. And, with the way the other passengers are quickly spreading word around that you are a famous novelist, Kate, the public appearance could help you sell a few books."

Marco had leaned forward listening intently as Casey spoke. He turned to Kate and raised his shoulders. "Kate, she's right. It would be fun and could be good publicity for you. I think we should do it."

"Practice will be held every afternoon between noon and 6:00 p.m. in the Karaoke Bar," Casey continued. "We will assign definite times to each couple, and there will be music available. You would compete in two different dances of your choice. The judges will be chosen from other passengers on the cruise. We can even help with your costumes. It has always been one of the favorite shows on our previous cruises. What do you think? Are you in?"

Kate and Marco looked at each other, then answered simultaneously, "Yes, we'll do it."

"That is fantastic! We've never had a celebrity participant before. This is going to be great. I'll put all the information about the competition in your mailboxes tomorrow morning. Thank you very much. You're going to be phenomenal!" Casey grinned as she walked away, but the excitement didn't feel mutual.

Oh great! What have I gotten myself into this time?

The next morning found Kate busily typing on her laptop. Handwritten notes were strewn all over the balcony table, weighed down by anything she could find in the suite to keep them from blowing in the wind from her open balcony door. The characters had almost reached the point of development where they took over the story, leaving her to merely type out the words.

At one of her book signings, she tried to explain to the readers that her characters were the ones developing the plot; she was only there to type the words. Their subsequent questions showed they didn't quite understand the concept. That was the last time Kate shared her writing secrets. She quietly laughed when she thought about what they'd think if she told them about Edward.

No, Edward would always be her personal secret.

Over the years, their relationship seemed to have changed. Edward became more demonstrative towards her. Thinking about the change, Kate was surprised at how much she enjoyed his tender touches and the feeling of his body close to her.

Just as quickly as the thought formed in her mind, Kate dismissed it. She knew Edward wasn't real. What she was feeling was only the product of dreams.

Come back to reality, old girl. You should just be happy that this book is finally moving along at a good pace. Stop indulging in fanciful feelings for someone who doesn't even exist.

Kate returned her thoughts to the book. So far, Millie was falling in love with Edward, and he seemed smitten with her. Lady Teresa had developed a friendship with the navigator, Henry, and they looked like they could be headed towards their own romance. Since Edward knew Sophia wasn't the royalty he sought, he allowed her to stay behind on the *Santa Magdalena* and instructed her to report back to the grand duke and duchess of all that had taken place on board.

All Kate had to do was come up with an idea for how the royal family could accept Henry as a potential suitor. The solution to that problem had come to her this morning while she was in the shower. Since she was in the faster phase of the free writing part of the book, she hoped to get that situation completed before lunch. This was the last sail day before they reached their first port: Grand Cayman Island.

A little before 1:00 p.m., Kate heard the suite door open and Ellie come in. They always had lunch together, then spent a little time shopping or walking around the deck before it was time to return to the suite. After lunch, Kate returned to her room to write for a while before she met Marco at five o'clock for their first dance practice. Ellie and Adam were going to an afternoon deck-side lecture on the Grand Cayman Island. Ellie had promised to take notes of anything that might interest her grandmother for use in the book. As soon as the door closed, Kate turned to her computer and began writing.

Chapter Five

THE FIERY PASSION OF A THOUSAND BURNING SUNS

Millie

The Falcon continued its journey to Edward's island home. Millie overheard Edward talking to his crew, saying that they planned to stay there for several days while repairs were made to the ship. He wanted the crew to have time to rest and feel the solid earth under their feet. His plan was to then take Millie and Lady Teresa back to England, while trying to avoid another kidnapping attempt by mutineers. There, he planned for the real Lady Teresa to be delivered unharmed to the grand duke.

Millie didn't mind being on the ship, regardless of the unexpected guests they now had leading the way. She loved the feel of the sea breeze and watching the porpoises playfully swim beside the ship as it cut through the water. Edward was still pressing her to reveal her true identity, but out of loyalty to Lady Teresa, she had not given in to his appeals. Millie knew that she and Lady Teresa would be taken back to Seville as soon as the ship was ready to leave the island, but she was not anxious to return. In the short time they had been together, Edward had shown so much patience and compassion with them that he had quickly stolen her heart. Her only desire was to be with him.

Soon they approached the island. Edward was right; the island was beautiful. He showed them to his home, showing a *level of trust that Millie hadn't realized they'd developed. How bad could Edward really be if he was willing to open his private home to them?*

The stone and palm wood house was comfortable, with individual bedrooms built around a large open living area. The rooms were sparsely furnished but clean, with windows across from each other that allowed for the cross ventilation of the consistent sea breeze. The beds had wooden frames held together by crisscrossed ropes covered by a large goose-down mattress. Native flowers bloomed in vibrant colors outside along the walk leading to the house. Large clay pots holding larger plants were placed on a small patio that led into the living area of the house. Millie had never seen any place so beautiful. Seeing Edward's island and home, she felt a tug of longing in her heart to live somewhere so stunning and peaceful. Millie headed out to the beach to explore more of the lush island.

"Ye must take care of the sun," Edward called to her. "Ye not be wanting to get a burn."

"I'll be careful. It's just so beautiful on the beach." She headed back towards the house to where he stood, his tall form leaning casually against the open doorframe. "Your home is perfect. I love the flowers and all the fruit trees. You must enjoy the time you are able to spend in this paradise."

"Aye, lassie, that I do. I be having everything a man could want here. The afternoon rains provide us with needed water. The trees and the sea provide us with food, so we have no other needs." Edward paused and winked at her before adding, "I mean, no other needs for food or water. With you around, I'll always have needs."

She giggled and playfully waved him away, then continued her exploration around the house and garden. As she walked, she started to get a feel for how the island was laid out. It was divided into designated spaces, starting with Edward's main house then fanning out to other smaller buildings that served as homes for his crew. The men with families lived on one side of the island in individual dwellings, while the unmarried members of the crew lived on the other side in buildings that housed up to four men each. There was a fenced area for the crew members' children and a communal fire pit kitchen.

Edward told her that their days at home were spent with everyone either fishing or gathering the abundant fruits in the surrounding forest. When enough food had been gathered or caught, the group cut the fish into pieces, lightly covered them with salt, and left everything in the full sun to dry. The vegetables and fruit were placed in a solution of salt brine and stored in crocks. Other supplies had been brought to the island on the ship and were placed in the larder located in a cool spot in the shade of a grove of palm trees.

After the supplies were replenished, the time was right for merriment.

Millie watched as a big feast was prepared throughout the afternoon, full of various savory dishes made ready by the women of the group. The men contributed many bottles of rum that were placed on the long rustic table in the yard. As the sun disappeared from view, lanterns were lit, and the fun began. The crew and their families all sat around the table, eating to their fill and drinking a little more than their fill. Children happily ran around anxiously awaiting the time the grown-ups finished and the baskets of dulces, or sweets, would be passed around.

Millie sat next to Edward with Lady Teresa and Henry beside them. Lady Teresa seemed to be fascinated by all the activity and Henry's company. All in all, it was a festive party. Millie couldn't believe how carefree and simple life was on the island.

She looked at Edward. "You have a wonderful life here. Is it difficult to leave when you have to go to sea?"

"Nay, I think if I be having a woman here it could be hard to leave. Alone, I find that when I be on land for a time, the sea calls for me to return. It be better this time, since ye be here with me." Edward reached over and took Millie's hand in his.

His hand felt warm and sure in hers. She reveled in the touch of his skin against hers; the roughness of his calloused palm on her smooth one. "I'm glad, Edward. I think I could live here forever as long as you were by my side. I love everything about this island and this place." Looking directly into Edward's eyes, Millie repeated, "I truly love everything here."

Edward's deep green eyes bored into hers. "Why don't we return to me house? We be leaving in just two short days, and the sea dinnae provide near as nice rest as me home."

Millie smiled demurely, knowing that Edward had other things on his mind than rest. They stood from the table, bidding goodnight to their friends, and walked hand in hand back to the house.

"Have you noticed how well Henry and the other girl are getting along?" Millie asked, careful not mention Lady Teresa by name.

"Aye, I be thinking that Henry might be serious about her."

"Well, if the real Lady Teresa were to fall in love with a man from a pirate ship and wanted to marry him, what do you think the grand duke would say?"

"That be a hard question. I believe the grand duke to be an honorable man. Since his niece be rescued from a difficult fate by other pirates, he might be inclined to give his blessing. Why ye be asking?"

"No reason, just curiosity, I guess."

They reached the house, and Millie's heart sped up in her chest, beating wildly with the anticipation of being alone with Edward.

Chapter Six

*K*ate stopped at that point and took a little break from her writing. She rubbed her eyes, then looked out at the sea. An emotion rose in her that she couldn't quite name.

The book was moving along, and Edward seemed to have found someone he was happy with. However, she wondered if her readers would be pleased by Edward's new love or whether they would prefer him to stay unattached in order to have more adventures in future books. She knew they clamored for a happily ever after, but would a happily ever after ring true in their hearts for the beloved Captain Peregrine?

Even though she tried to keep the thought from her mind, she couldn't help but wonder how she felt about Edward's new love. She and Edward had worked together so closely in the last few years that she had gotten used to him belonging to her. He was a figment of her imagination only. No one else shared the conversations she did with him, or the laughs, or the playful touches. Now, he seemed taken with Millie. Kate realized that the thought of Edward finding true love and leaving her was more than she could bear. What would she do without the comfort of his company?

After a few moments, she glanced at her watch and realized she had been lost in her thoughts a little longer than she realized. It was getting close to time to meet Marco.

Focus, Kate. There is a real man showing real interest in you. Let Edward stay in his story and go write one for yourself.

She stood up from the chair and headed inside from the balcony to get dressed for their dance practice. She ignored the nagging fear that followed her.

After some discussion, Marco and Kate chose the two dances they would perform in the contest. The first was a lively rendition of the Charleston, a dance popular in the time of flappers and speakeasies. The other was a smoldering tango.

Kate didn't feel too confident in her abilities to convey smoldering at this point in her life, but Marco assured her that she could still melt the snowcaps of Alaska. She enjoyed dancing with him, the way their bodies moved together in synchronized steps. But it wasn't just the dancing that made her time with Marco enjoyable. She also loved when they sat together on the deck, watching the rolling waves of the sparkling Caribbean waters, and just talked. He was a good listener and seemed genuinely interested in her and her work. It had been a long time since Kate had been with someone as relaxed and caring as Marco. She began to wonder if maybe she might have finally met someone who would help her find her lost feelings of love and passion.

As Kate entered the theater, Marco was waiting. He greeted her with a kiss on the cheek.

"Kate, I'm happy to see you. I have worked out the choreography for our dances."

Kate sat next to him at a small table, where they reviewed his notes for the dance.

"I thought we would each enter from different sides of the stage and use the quick steps to slowly move to the middle and move on to the more complicated moves. The most difficult part will be where we face each other, hold hands while stepping back, and then give a little kick as we move closer together again. We might need shin guards while we practice that one."

"Marco!" Kate exclaimed in mock indignation. "You know I would never kick you in the shin—at least not hard enough that you would need protection."

Marco raised his eyebrows and grinned. "Could I get that in writing, please?"

Returning to the overview, Marco went over the order of the dances and all the steps. Sometimes he stood up to demonstrate a particular dance move. Kate listened intently, trying to remember everything he said and showed her.

Finally, it was time for them to begin the practice. Kate resisted the urge to bite at her fingernails as they began rehearsing the Charleston. After they worked out the timing and stage position, the practice went flawlessly and Kate's nerves faded away. Marco had that effect on her.

The tango proved to be a little more difficult. There were a lot of missed steps. She laughed when she realized how many times she apologized to Marco for stepping on his toes or accidentally kicking his shin.

After the last assault on his toes, Marco looked at his watch. With a sigh of relief and an accompanying smile, he said, "The gods must be on my side; our allotted time is up."

Kate laughed. "Let me help you back to your cabin."

"A true Italian man never admits defeat by a woman. I'd rather crawl back to my cabin myself in martyrdom." Marco flashed her a disarming smile then took her hand and kissed it.

The happy duo left the theater to return to their cabins and get ready for dinner.

The conversation at the dinner table centered around plans for the first port day on Grand Cayman Island. Kate remembered from a previous visit that Grand Cayman, the largest of the three Cayman Islands, was surrounded by a coral reef system. Because of the reefs and shallow water around the island, the ship's passengers would need to be tendered to the island. The tour excursions brochure mentioned that the island was a diver's paradise with sunken shipwrecks, grottos, and steep underwater walls.

Although Kate and Ellie had planned their shore excursions in advance, Ellie asked her earlier in the day if it would be all right to branch off and do some things with Adam. Kate didn't mind, happy to allow her granddaughter some time with someone her own age that she seemed to be hitting it off with. Now that inspiration had struck, Kate was looking forward to a quiet day of writing anyway.

So, with Kate's blessing, Ellie would take Adam with her on their "Swim with the Dolphins" tour. The Andersons and David decided on a "Best of the Island" tour that would give them a wonderful overview of the area. Marco and Bettina would be staying on board. The dinner ended and everyone decided to retire early in anticipation of the first day on shore.

Kate awoke the next morning to sounds of the lifeboat tenders beginning their runs, taking passengers to the individual excursions. Walking out to the balcony, she could see all the tour buses lined up, waiting to show their island paradise to the visiting tourists. Sitting there and watching all the excited passengers on their way to various excursions, she was a little disappointed not to be going on a tour. The colorful buildings and white sands contrasted with the exquisite turquoise of the Caribbean Sea. The more she watched all the activity, the more she wanted to be on shore.

After a light breakfast, Kate went to the customer service area and inquired whether there might be an opening for the afternoon city tour. To her good fortune, there was an opening on one of the later buses. Rather than feeling guilty for neglecting Edward, Kate was giddy with anticipation for the opportunity to tour this city once again.

The tender took Kate to the staging area used for all shore excursions. After a quick glance around at the signs, she found her tour and boarded the bus. As she walked down the aisle, she heard someone call her name. Kate looked around and was surprised to see David and the Andersons sitting a few rows back. David motioned to the empty seat beside him. She made her way down the narrow aisle of the luxury tour bus and sat next to him.

He smiled. "Hey, we didn't think you were going on any tours. Glad to see you changed your mind."

Kate laughed. "The town just looked too inviting to pass up, so I decided to play hooky from work today and see what Grand Cayman has to offer."

Oscar and Amanda, seated behind them, leaned forward and told her that they were happy she joined the tour.

"You're here at just the right time, too," Oscar said. "This is the beginning of the eleven-day long 'Pirates Week.'"

Amanda added, "Who knows, it might be someplace that Captain Peregrine could visit on his next adventure."

Kate was thrilled to learn that the event would be in full swing. She had heard of Pirates Week but had forgotten when it was.

Oscar continued, "I understand that they turn the place into an eighteenth-century pirate encampment, complete with mock invasions, parades, costumes, and lots of food and drink."

"Kate," David said, "I think your pirate must have subconsciously sent you a message to go on this tour just so you could see how people lived during his time. I'm sure you'll find something you can add to your book."

Kate just smiled as she secretly thanked Edward, just in case he actually was responsible for her changing her mind about the tour.

Before long, the air-conditioned bus started their four-hour journey. The tour guide recounted stories and highlights of the Grand Cayman Island to the group. They drove by the governor's mansion and then made a quick stop at the Old Homestead, more commonly known as the Pink House. The tour guide explained that the Old Homestead was one of the oldest houses on the island, built in 1912, and was typical of the colonial era homes of that period.

Next, they visited the world famous "Hell." David explained that Hell consisted of short, black limestone formations protruding from the ground caused by biological erosion that resembled what some people had described as Hell. The area was a must-see for tourists. Even though it was small, there was a Devil's Hangout gift shop and a post office where visitors could send postcards back home with a postmark letting the recipient know that the sender had mailed the card from Hell. They happily explored the walkways around the exquisite rock formations. David snapped pictures at every turn in the walk.

Soon the tour guide announced it was time to make their way to the reconstructed pirate encampment for a glimpse of life in the 1700s. On the way to the event, David pointed out a group of reproduction pirate ships heading towards the island that appeared to be part of a flotilla. When the tour reached the destination, everyone rushed off the bus and hurried down to the landing where the ships were tying up. By the time they reached the wharf, Kate could make out men on each ship all dressed as pirates and looking as menacing as possible to the enjoyment of the audience.

The pirates left the ships and mingled with the tourists, taking pictures and playfully waving their pirate swords menacingly at any woman who walked by. Amanda pointed out a group of children around five or six years old dressed in pirate costumes and carrying wooden flintlock-type pistols and swords. They were playfully attacking the pirates and joining in singing, "Yo ho, yo ho, a pirates' life for me." It was a song Kate remembered well from her trips with the grandchildren to Disney World. The whole scene was lively. The pirates were pretty realistic, although Kate thought that there wasn't a one of them who could even come close to being as rakish as Edward. She and the others strolled around the encampment stopping at the various shops before finally settling for an outdoor cafe selling grog and small sandwiches of dried pork and bread with condiments of choice.

Heading out on their own, David continued taking more pictures as he and Kate explored the whole area. All during the walk, he had been very attentive, taking her hand when they walked over rocks and bumpy terrain. The scenery was magnificent, and the company was even better. She was so glad she had decided to come. She had taken quite a few notes on things she could use later in the book. All in all, it had been an amazing afternoon.

She was so tired on the ride back to the staging area with all the walking they had done that the gentle swaying of the bus relaxed her. It wasn't long before she dozed off. When she awoke, she was surprised and a little flustered when she realized her head had fallen onto David's shoulder. Even though he was still asleep himself, head resting against the window, she pulled back quickly, putting space between them. She didn't think he was the type who would mind, but it was awkward to wake up with her head on his shoulder. Even if it was fairly normal for seniors to fall asleep after any type of exertion. With that thought, she looked around the bus and noticed that almost all the passengers were dozing, including the younger members of the tour. The brief anxiety she felt faded quickly.

Dinner that night was exciting. Everyone wanted to recount the experiences of the day. Kate was afraid that Marco and Bettina would feel left out, but he assured them that they would learn more about the island if everyone talked about the tours.

"I can't believe that after years of waiting, I finally got to swim with the dolphins," Ellie gushed, grinning as she jumped in her seat. The excitement seemed like it hadn't worn off for her quite yet.

"It really was incredible," Adam agreed. "Though I didn't expect how…rubbery they would feel."

"Better than slimy, like I always thought," Ellie said. "After the dolphins, we went to check out the pirate week fun and tried diving for treasure. Adam, did you bring the bag?"

Adam nodded and pulled a few items out of their bag of treasure. They passed around some gold-painted Spanish eight-reale coins they had found.

Kate smiled as she watched them interact. She'd never seen her granddaughter so giddy around one of her boyfriends. It was sweet to watch young love blossom. Their enthusiasm for each other gave her more ideas for the kind of new love she wanted Millie and Edward to experience.

Everyone acknowledged that the beautiful turquoise and blue waters of the Caribbean added to the enjoyment of the excursions. They couldn't have been there at a better time.

"Take a look at some of these pictures." David pulled out his camera and clicked through. He leaned over to Marco and Bettina, tilting the screen so they could see all the pictures he took. "Look at how beautiful and colorful the island was. And the creatures you could see through the crystal-clear waters. Isn't it stunning? I plan to share these with some of my friends in the Latin American, marine biology, and history departments. There's a little something for everyone, don't you think? Even the geologists might be fascinated by these rock formations…" David trailed off, mumbling to himself about the different academic aspects of a cruise as Marco described his day.

"While Bettina was napping, I relaxed on one of the comfortable couches on the deck, just watching the water and all the brightly painted tenders and leisure boats going back and forth. All the tourism activity made me tired just watching." Marco didn't look disappointed in the slightest that he missed out on all the island had to offer. He seemed happy everyone had enjoyed their day.

After dinner, Marco stood from his chair first and offered his hand to Kate, who was still seated. "Shall we?" She smiled and nodded, so they headed to the Salsa Bar for a little dancing. Although he smiled all through dinner, he seemed unusually quiet on the way to the lounge. When they hit the dance floor, his heart didn't seem to be in the music.

After the first dance, Kate gently leaned toward him. "Are you okay? We don't have to dance tonight if you're tired."

"No, I'm just a little distracted by the upcoming meeting in Cartagena, and Bettina had a pretty rough day today. She just seems to be getting worse. I don't know what to do." Marco's voice cracked a little, and he quickly turned his head away.

She took his hand and murmured, "Marco, if there's one thing I've learned in life, it is to try and not worry about what could or might happen. There is a strong possibility that your meeting will go well and everything will work out just fine for Bettina's treatment. Then all the time wasted worrying would be for naught. Take each day at a time and worry only about realities, not possibilities. You have friends on the ship, and we will support you through your problems."

"Kate, you are a wonder. I cannot even begin to imagine how I would have managed this trip without you being here. It is very odd that I feel so close to you when we have only just met. You feel like a cherished friend and a supportive partner. I appreciate your willingness to provide aid and comfort to me in my time of need." Marco took Kate's hand and looked deep into her eyes. "I have never in my life ever asked anyone for help with anything, but you are so kind and loving I almost feel that I could depend on you if I ever needed someone."

"Of course, you can depend on me, Marco. That is what people do for one another. That's what makes us human." Kate gently laid her hand on his arm to comfort him.

Marco laid his hand over hers and looked away again. He pulled a handkerchief out of his pocket and dabbed his eyes, then put the cloth back in his pocket. When he looked back at her, a big smile transformed his face. "It's time we dance. Hold on, Kate. We're going to clear the floor."

And they did.

Later, Kate entered the suite to find Ellie already settled in for the night. She had ordered chocolate covered strawberries and a pot of hot tea that had just arrived. Already in her pajamas, she was watching one of the five or six film noirs the ship played through its limited in-house, closed-circuit TV.

"Grandma!" Ellie exclaimed. "You got here just in time. Our favorite film is playing—for the fourth time."

Kate glanced at the screen and saw Charles Boyer looking very sinister in *Gaslight*. She kicked off her shoes and collapsed on the couch next to Ellie, immediately reaching for a strawberry.

"So, how did your date go with David?" Ellie asked.

"Date? With David? We just happened to be on the same city tour, along with Adam's parents. It wasn't a date." Kate watched the TV for a moment, then added, "Although, something funny did happen. On the way back from the tour, David and I, along with almost every other person on the bus, fell asleep. I flopped over and had my head resting on his shoulder. I felt a little embarrassed at first, but he was extremely nice about the whole thing. He said he barely even noticed because he'd been asleep too. Though he did say it was nice to have a woman rest her head on him again."

"Aha," Ellie chided. "So, you were sleeping with David in the afternoon, dancing with Marco this evening, and I can only imagine what you will do if Edward comes to your bedroom tonight. What kind of example are you setting for your innocent granddaughter?"

Kate laughed, picked up a pillow, and threw it at Ellie. She narrowly missed knocking over Ellie's cup of tea. "I wasn't sleeping with David. I was sleeping and my head rolled over. David is a very nice man, and I hope he becomes a good friend."

"Okay. Protest all you want, but I think I've got a geriatric Jezebel for a grandmother." Ellie reached over and picked up a strawberry while she raised her eyebrows and grinned at her grandmother.

"Eleanor Elizabeth Caldwell, you're not too old to be sent to your room. Besides, what about you and Adam? You've been spending a lot of time together. What's up with that?"

At the mention of Adam's name, a light blush rose in Ellie's cheeks. "Adam is really nice. We like the same things, we laugh a lot, and we're both at the same place in our lives. I'm really enjoying spending time with him. He's making plans for us to do things when we get back, so he may be around a lot. At least, I hope he stays around."

"Looks like I'm not the only Jezebel." Kate winked at her granddaughter before standing up and stretching. "Enjoy the movie. I think I'm going to bed so I can try to get some writing done in the morning." Kate glanced at the TV and added, "Just so you know, I think Charles Boyer is trying to drive Ingrid Bergman crazy."

"Sounds good. Oh, I know you've been worrying about Marco and Bettina, but Adam and I saw them when we went by Adam's room to put up his wet swim trunks. Their room is right across from the Andersons' and Bettina looked well. She and Marco were laughing and whispering when they went into the room. They didn't see us, and we didn't want to interrupt them so we didn't say anything. But they seemed to be doing okay today."

Kate smiled, relieved to hear some good news about Marco and Bettina. "That's good. Marco has really been worried about her so I'm glad they seemed happy. Don't stay up too late. Good night."

Chapter Seven

$\mathcal{K}$ate woke during the night to find Edward sitting on her bed, staring at her. "Edward, you almost scared me half to death," she nearly shouted, while pulling the covers up to her chin. "Let me know when you are in my room."

"Sorry, Kate, ye just looked so peaceful that I dinnae want to wake ye."

"Did you have an idea for the story?" she asked, heart rate slowly coming back down to a normal rhythm.

"Not really. Everything ye have written so far has been pleasing." He hesitated, rubbing the back of his neck, before he continued. "I do have one little complaint though. I know ye cannae hear me when ye be awake, but if ye be writing and me and a lady seem to be moving towards an intimate moment, will ye not stop typing during that time? Ye know that I cannae be doing anything ye have not written before, so that be putting me in a rather…delicate situation. I not be saying that I think ye do this purposeful but just wanted ye to understand."

"Oh, Edward, I am so sorry," Kate replied, just a hint of sarcasm in her voice. "Did I do that to you? You do know it wasn't intentional, don't you?"

Edward laughed. "Katie girl, we both be full of blarney, but I forgive ye this time. I think the girl I will have feelings for is the first girl I questioned when we boarded. I cannae but think she really be the handmaiden and Lady Teresa be the other one. It does appear the lady be getting a little smitten with Henry. Maybe ye could write something about their romance."

"That's a great idea. I'll work on that angle tomorrow. What else have you come up with?"

Edward paused again. He hesitated longer this time, his face morphing into a serious expression she had never seen on him before. "Kate, sometimes there be handsome ships sailing on the seas that people cannae help but appreciate for their sleekness and beauty. However, many times the ship be flying a false flag of deception and is not what it appears. Be careful and make sure the ship ye fancy be flying a true flag."

"I'm not sure what you are referencing, but I'll be careful." She felt herself drifting back into a deep slumber just as he leaned down to brush the hair from her forehead. She thought she felt the warmth of his gentle kiss on her cheek as he whispered, "G'night, Katie girl. I pray ye have smooth sailing."

The next port of call was Aruba. Kate had visited the island many times before and decided to opt out of a shore excursion, for real this time, to stay on the ship and write. She also needed a little time alone so she could put her thoughts in order. Kate took notes, but most of the book played out visually in her head, like a movie playing. Someone had once told her that she had inner vision, and that did seem to be true. She couldn't put the words down until she viewed the whole scene, and that required alone time, or "brain download time."

She went out on the balcony to gaze at the beautiful island with its wonderful beaches and glorious clear blue waters. The breathtaking view gave her a perfect opportunity to reflect on the trip so far and her friendship with Marco. Kate enjoyed the attention he showered on her and was beginning to realize just how lonely these past few years had been. It wasn't until she started dancing with Marco that she realized how much she missed the touch of a man. She was not the type of woman who was meant to live a loveless life; there was a yearning in her heart to be happily paired with someone who would always be there to take her hand or hold her in his arms.

Although she knew her children and grandchildren greatly loved her, she longed for another kind of love; the kind that could only be shared between two people who were genuinely committed to each other. In recent years, she had begun to feel angry and cheated that she had been denied the very comfort she so desired. Even watching Hallmark movies made her bitter and teary-eyed when the couples kissed and lived happily ever after. But there was something on this cruise that made her feel different. She wondered if maybe her dreams would come to fruition. Marco seemed so vulnerable because of Bettina's illness, but he stayed strong. Instead of dwelling on his problems, he made sure Kate was happy. Men like that didn't come along very often.

As Kate reflected on Marco and their time together, she found her thoughts drifting to one of the most fun days she'd had so far—with David. She thought about the shore excursion and how he was so excited about everything they had seen, how he included her in his various discoveries, and how comforting his shoulder was when she had fallen asleep on the bus. If Marco had not been on the cruise, would David pursue her? Would they have a friendship?

Then, her thoughts turned to Edward. He wasn't real, but she had always accepted his existence. Their friendship deepened with each visit. His gentle touch and recent good-night kisses seemed to suggest that he might be developing feelings for her. What had he meant by someday belongs to us? With the thoughts of Edward taking over her brain, Kate stood from the chair and paced around the room as she talked to herself.

"Kate Caldwell, are you crazy? Why do you keep thinking about Edward, just a product of your imagination, like he is a real person? You are losing it, old girl. Time to open your laptop and start on some real work."

With that, she took a seat in front of her computer once more and started writing.

Chapter Eight

THE FIERY PASSION OF A THOUSAND BURNING SUNS

Sophia

The plundered Santa Magdalena *arrived in the port of South-ampton. Sophia was glad to be back in her country but dreaded telling the grand duke and duchess that Lady del Gado had been kidnapped. She feared they would hold her responsible.*

After tying up to their mooring, Sophia walked down the gangplank to leave the ship. As she made her way to the dock, she saw a large and ornate black carriage waiting on the pier. The conveyance was intended for Lady Teresa. After taking a couple of deep breaths, Sophia determinedly walked straight to the carriage, knowing her job was to inform everyone of the kidnapping and to offer as much information as possible. As she got closer, she could see the captain of the ship speaking to the grand duke, which eased her anxiety a little. At least the grand duke would already be informed about Lady Teresa's fate.

As Sophia walked closer, she heard her name being called. "Sophia, come quickly, child. I want to know all the facts of Lady Teresa's capture."

Sophia ran to the carriage and politely stood before Lady Teresa's uncle.

"Sophia, I need to know who the pirate was that captured my niece. Do you know what ship he sailed?"

"Yes, Your Grace, I know the ship. It was the Falcon and the captain was Edward Peregrine." As she spoke, Sophia reached in the pocket of her dress, pulled out a piece of paper, and handed it to the grand duke. "Captain Peregrine gave me a dispatch to give to you."

"Oh, thanks be to God. I had hoped that it would be he. At least we know that Lady Teresa is safe and he will do no harm to her."

"He was an imposing man, Your Grace, but we came up with a plan to trick him so that he wouldn't know which one was Lady Teresa. Lady Teresa dressed in Millie's clothing, and we all covered our hair. The captain quickly discovered my subterfuge when he removed the snood and saw the dark color of my hair compared to theirs, but he did seem truly confused between Millie and Lady Teresa. He told them he would discover their true identities during the voyage. I was so scared that he might throw me overboard when he found that I was not worthy of a ransom, but he kindly told me I would be sent back, and no harm would come to me." Sophia began to cry. "I'm so sorry, Your Grace. We tried to protect her, but we couldn't. I begged to stay with her, but the captain said I had to leave. I don't know what will become of me now."

"There, there, my dear child." The grand duke gently patted her head. "Take my arm and climb aboard the carriage. I know you did your best, but you could not be expected to fend off the likes of Captain Peregrine. Climb aboard the carriage, and we will return to the manor. You will take care of Lady Teresa's belongings and her room until her return." He held his arm out to help her into the carriage.

"Thank you, Your Grace. I kept her jewelry box locked and in my possession the whole voyage home." Sophia proudly handed the box over to the grand duke.

"Excellent job, Sophia. You have proven yourself worthy."

She climbed into the carriage, happy in the knowledge that she would still have her job with the family. As the mules began to pull the coach away from the dock, she looked back with sadness in her heart and wondered if Lady Teresa and Millie were all right.

❧

Millie

The day had proven majestic. Fluffy white clouds still dotted a deepening blue sky, and a gentle breeze flowed through the sails. The Falcon navigated smoothly through the waters of the Caribbean Sea, leaving the secluded island and heading north to the Atlantic. Millie relaxed lazily on the aft deck, enjoying the warmth of the midday sun while admiring the exquisite blue-green color of the water. She heard Edward approaching and turned to smile at him as he sat beside her.

"It is very beautiful here. I can see why you love to be on the water." She looked back at the sea, gazing at the beauty of the waters around her, before looking back at him. "Edward, why did you become a pirate? You have not the manners of the usual blackards who roam the sea, stealing from ships and terrorizing the crew and passengers. You have the genteel manners of a man of honor."

"Aye, 'tis a long story that I not often be telling, but with you, I be willing to share me tale. Me father was a Scotsman and me brother, Norman, who be three years older than me, and I be raised in that country. After the death of me grandfather, who built a shipping business in England, we moved there so me father could take over the business. Me brother and I worked with him, sailing the merchant ships to ports around the world while me father managed the business."

Edward's voice deepened and he looked away as he continued. "In that time, we be seeing the problems of people in the Caribbean and in South America, and how they be taken advantage of by the Spanish government and the House of Commerce in Seville. The colonists be taxed heavily and much of the countries' natural resources of silver, gold, and precious gems be stolen from them to take back to Spain aboard the large Spanish galleons."

He cleared his throat, and when he continued, Millie could hear a little more gruffness in his voice. She placed a hand on his knee and squeezed to let him know she was there. "When me father died, me brother took over running the company. I stayed at sea, determined to help make the lives of the poor people in the Caribbean a little better. Me crew and I, we overpower the galleons and take only half of their cargo. With what we take, we can give supplies and other aid to the people on the islands."

As he explained their method, the emotion seemed to drain from his voice. In its place, a certain determination came through, as if he was desperate to make people understand he wasn't a bad man and wasn't hurting anyone. "We do not fight unless we are attacked. We use speed, skill, and the threat of our cannons to convince the boats to surrender to our boarding. The English and Spanish governments know what it is we do and mostly do not come after us. Spain feels that we be discouraging other pirates from going after a ship we have set sail for. By us giving quarter to the crew and only taking half of the cargo, they be faring better than with other pirates."

Millie leaned against his shoulder, more comfortable than ever in his presence. "So, you really are like the legendary Robin Hood, gallantly robbing from the rich to give to the poor."

"'Tis not quite that romantic. We only be trying to help people who be having a difficult time, and since the land be theirs, it is only fair."

"What about your mother? Were you close to her?"

A deep sadness washed over his face. She ached to take that face in her hands and kiss every evidence of sadness—the downturn of his mouth, the furrow in his brows, the faint tears in his eyes.

"Me mother was a beautiful lady," he said. "She be from Ireland and a part of the Black Irish, but her eyes were as green as the Emerald Isle itself. She be a good mother and a good wife to me father. When I reached me eighteenth birthday, she caught a chill and died from pneumonia two weeks later. Me father be stuck in a deep sorrow after that. He be never truly recovered from her death."

Millie took his hand in hers. "I am very sorry, Edward. That must have been hard on your family."

Edward squeezed her hand but didn't reply. The two sat side by side on the deck looking up as the fiery clouds from the setting sun blazed across the sky. He stood and helped her to her feet, suggesting they go to the cabins before the light of the day left the sky.

As they entered the main cabin, Lady Teresa and Henry were deeply engrossed in studying Henry's new Davis's quadrant. He was explaining how this invention helped a navigator measure the altitude of the sun, removing the need to look directly at it. When the sky was dark, they could go up on deck to study the constellations, and he would explain how to use the constellations to find their position. Lady Teresa seemed genuinely fascinated by what he was saying, so Edward suggested that he and Millie go to his cabin so as not to disturb the two stargazers. She was hesitant to go alone with him, especially since she knew royalty would never be caught alone in a room with a member of the opposite sex outside of marriage, but the thought of being with Edward overcame her reluctance. The more time they spent together, the more her defenses fell.

He led her back to his cabin in the stern of the ship. Though the room was small, Millie was surprised by the luxury of its decoration. The mahogany-paneled room held a desk with an hourglass, a quill, ink, and a logbook. A standing telescope stood next to a comfortable chair by three large windows. The wall to the right of the desk had a large bookcase filled with leather-bound books. On the other side of the room, there was a comfortable looking bed with a goose-down mattress and comforter. The room even had a small, colorful Persian rug on the floor. Heavy draperies were hung beside all the windows in the cabin giving the overall effect of an elegant bedchamber.

As they walked into the dimly lit room, Edward took Millie's hand and led her over to the window, where they could continue to watch the setting sun.

"I do not know who ye be, but ye be a beautiful, kindhearted woman. I be enjoying the time we spend together and feel a contentment when you be by me side that I not be feeling for many a day."

She could see the desire in his flirtatious eyes and feel the welcoming warmth of his body close to hers. They had held each other before but had never passed the point of no return. Tonight, Millie sensed something different. Edward was still tender and loving in his touch, but she could feel a strong longing in his manner. He gazed at her with a fiery passion in his eyes. He pulled her close to him and held her tightly, almost as if he were afraid she would leave and be lost to him forever.

She leaned her head against his shoulder and murmured, "Edward, I too have enjoyed our time and your company. When we are together, I feel a sense of contentment that I've never felt before."

He turned and gently took her face in his hands. He kissed her soundly on the lips. She wanted to resist him. She wanted to stay strong, to maintain their charade and step out of his arms, but with one kiss, her resolve faded. It was everything she had been longing for during these past few days, and she let herself relax in his touch. She yielded to the strength of his body, the tenderness of his touch, and the overwhelming need of his desire.

Slowly, he led her to the inviting bed. As she laid back in surrender to his spell, he drew her to him and began unfastening the buttons on her bodice. Even though she lay still beside him, her body felt a new and wondrous excitement. He removed his shirt to reveal taut muscles beneath the mass of hair covering *his chest. The moment was electric. Edward stared at the beauty of her body and began exploring her femininity with his hands. She felt like she was going to explode with happiness and threw her arms around him with a hunger that surprised them both.*

"Grandma, it's lunch time!"

Kate stopped typing when she heard Ellie enter the stateroom. "Is it one already? I've been so heads down typing that I didn't notice what time it was." Kate was ready to click on *Save* when something held her back. "Give me a few more minutes. I'm at a pivotal point in the plot and just want to finish this scene."

"That's fine. I want to look over the brochure for our shore excursion tomorrow."

Her passionate response seemed to make Edward want her more. He gently rolled on top of her while she guided him to her secret place of warmth. His heavy weight was comforting in a way she'd never felt with another man. Although her experience had been limited, it had never been like this. He moaned in pleasure above her as their bodies moved in a slow rhythm, the hardened buds of her bosom pressed firmly against his chest. They increased in intensity until they both breathlessly felt the sweet sensations of love's flowering release. She didn't want him to leave, despite the heaviness of his weight on her chest. When he moved, the cool air made her shiver as if she had lost something more important than she cared to admit.

But then he wrapped his arms around her and snuggled her into his embrace, and the feeling of loss drifted away.

For the first time in her life, she felt safe.

Nestled in his arms, Millie stroked his beard, letting her fingers lightly dance across the course hairs. The new pleasure she found in his arms did not fully erase the fear of him discovering her true identity. Would he still want her if he knew she wasn't royalty? Would he still love her, even if she was just Millie?

"Something troubling you? I hope I dinnae hurt ye," Edward said, brushing hair out of her face.

She shook her head and smiled up at him. "No. Everything is wonderful."

Millie pushed the thoughts away. She would not dwell on such things at this moment. His desire to hold her far outweighed any doubts she had.

Chapter Nine

"Grandma!" Ellie had walked out on the balcony and was looking over her shoulder at the computer. "Congratulations! After almost three books, you finally let Edward get laid. Good job. But what are 'the hardened buds of her bosom' and 'love's flowering release'? Are those metaphors for her nipples and an orgasm?"

"Elle! I can't use those words in my books. It's bad enough I had to describe the scene instead of just hinting at what was happening. Using words like you just said would be a little too crass for me."

"What words? You mean you can't say nipple?" Ellie laughed.

"Ellie, stop saying that word."

"What word?"

"The N word." Ellie was teasing her, and Kate knew it would go on for quite some time despite her exasperation. She resisted the impulse to roll her eyes.

"Grandma, that most definitely is not the N word. You can say nipple. Just don't think about it and quickly blurt out nipple, nipple, nipple."

"Eleanor, that is enough. There are ways to say things without being coarse or vulgar."

"Vulgar? Grandma, it's just body parts. Can you say elbow or leg or fingers?"

"Of course."

"Then nipple is the same thing—just a body part. What

word are you going to use to describe a man's sex organ—a wee wee?"

Kate looked down and put her face in her hands as she tried not to laugh at Ellie's last comment. Pretending to be annoyed, she straightened her features, looked up, and in a voice that had only a pretense of seriousness said, "Young lady, ever since you graduated college you have been a little cheeky, but today, you've moved up to irredeemable. Let's go to lunch before I put you in time out."

Ellie laughed and shrugged, leaning against the balcony railing. After all their years of teasing each other, Kate knew Ellie could tell she was just a little non-plussed over the scene she had just written.

Kate saved her work and carried the laptop over to the desk. As she entered the living space, she stopped and sniffed the air. The scent of cloves and cinnamon mixed with the distinct notes of patchouli.

"What's wrong?" Ellie asked, following her inside. "Do you smell something weird?"

"It's crazy, but I thought I smelled pipe tobacco when I closed the laptop."

"Not unusual. Edward is probably having an after-sex pipe."

Kate laughed and shook her head. "Maybe Millie is having one too. I really can't believe she was so quick to jump into bed with him. And Edward, what was he thinking? He's a little old to be cavorting around with the likes of a young girl like Millie. He really needs someone a little more mature and not so free with her favors."

"Grandma, Edward only does the things you write for him. The same with Millie. How can you criticize them for doing what you had them do?"

"Well, I just think he could do better if he just had a little patience."

"Grandma, if I didn't know better, I would think you are jealous of Millie." Ellie nudged Kate with her elbow and raised her eyebrows. "Maybe you have a little crush on Edward yourself. Do I need to chaperone the two of you when he comes to you in your room at night?"

Kate rolled her eyes and stepped away, throwing her hands in the air. "Elle, that is crazy. I created Edward. He is nothing more than a character in my imagination that manifests itself through my dreams. I just thought he might have had a little more sense than to jump into bed with a girl like her."

Ellie clucked her tongue and began singing, "Grandma and Edward sitting in a tree, K-I-S-S-I-N-G. First comes love, then comes marriage, then comes baby in a baby carriage!"

Kate reached out and playfully pulled her granddaughter towards the door. As she turned to close the door, Kate again got a whiff of pipe tobacco. The aroma seemed to annoy her more than it should.

After lunch, Kate came back to her room ready for a little quiet time before meeting Marco in the ship's theater to practice their dances. There was a light rain outside, and the sky was overcast. Ellie and Adam were going to the game room and then watching a movie, so Kate had the suite to herself. As she kicked off her Garavani sandals and stretched out on her bed, the gentle rock of the ship and the rain on the balcony lulled her into a deep sleep.

"Kate, I want to thank ye for the writing ye did today."

"Edward, I'm surprised to see you now." She rubbed her eyes and squinted at him where he stood at the foot of her bed. "You've never visited during the day."

"Aye, ye were sleeping so soundly I was able to come to ye."

"Why are you here? I thought you'd be with your little girlfriend," she responded with more than a hint of sarcasm.

"Katie girl, ye seem upset. Have I done something to offend ye?"

"I hardly think a figment of my imagination could possibly offend me. I am just a little surprised by your actions with Millie. It certainly didn't take you long to hop in bed with her."

Edward held his hands out in front of him, palms up. "Kate, this be a book. We dinnae have much time for long courtships. Besides, it was ye who had me hop into bed with the girl. Ye wrote the scene. I was an innocent partner." His voice had gotten noticeably louder and had a slight edge to it.

She could tell he was getting irritated with the conversation, but she continued. "Well, if you had any decency, you would've at least found out her name before bedding her. Or maybe I'm wrong about you. Maybe you aren't a decent man. Maybe you really are a scoundrel!"

Hurt washed over Edward's face as he took a step back and crossed his arms over his chest. "Kate, ye be unfair. Why does this girl bother ye so? Ye have had me pursue other women before and haven't been bothered. What is different this time?"

"Edward, you made love to her!" Kate shouted. "With the others, it was just suggested, but with this one, it actually happened."

His eyes widened and he threw his hands in the air. "Kate, it happened because ye made it happen."

She took a deep breath and turned her head away from him. In a barely audible whisper, she confessed, "I know. It just scares me that you have someone now. You and I have been together for three years. Even though I know you are a dream, I've gotten used to seeing you and being with you while we write our books. Now, I'm so afraid you'll leave me because you don't have a need for me anymore."

Edward walked across the room to sit on the edge of the bed next to her. He placed a hand under her chin and gently turned her head towards him. Their eyes met, his handsome face blurred through the tears in her eyes. He wiped the glistening drops that had already rolled down her cheeks.

"Aye, Katie girl. It be true that we be together for more than three years now, and over the time, I have come to feel a warmth for ye that has been growing with each visit. We work together well and seem to be having the same ideas and feelings about most things. Ye have become very important to me. I love the excitement ye feel for the books. I love the way I feel when I be with ye and we are working side by side on new stories as one. I love the kind way ye have with people and the care ye show family. I love the way ye worry about me, even though we be centuries apart. I love the gentleness and vulnerability of ye soul.

"With the time we be together and all the qualities ye possess, I have come to feel a love for ye that is as deep as the stars be high. There will never be a day in all of time that I won't need ye. Our bodies, minds, and souls fit together like perfectly matched pieces of an exquisite picture puzzle. There will come other people in our lives who seem to be a match. When we be with those people, they give us happiness, but they dinnae make the right picture. You and I be the perfect fit. When we be joined, we be completing a beautiful scene.

"Katie girl, we be destined to be together, but our time is not now. Ye have a life in this world, and I have a life in mine, but someday, it will be just the two of us. The life we be having then will be more splendid than ye can dream. Until that day, we must find happiness with people who almost be perfect. Ye soon will be having someone, and I be having Millie. But, Katie girl, ye hold me heart in your hands and me soul in your body. The love I be feeling for ye is not just for a moment in time; it is for eternity, and I will never leave you. Rest now, me girl, for a busy time be coming. Remember what I said about false flags."

Edward leaned down and softly kissed Kate's cheek before he faded from her vision. She fell back into a welcome sleep.

Chapter Ten

At precisely 4:30 p.m., Kate's alarm sounded, waking her in time to meet Marco. Their dance practice went well. Marco seemed in especially good spirits due to his upcoming meeting in Cartagena. He told Kate he was very optimistic about the outcome, and that all his problems would soon be solved. Kate was happy for him, but Edward's reassuring visit had done more to lift her spirits than being with Marco.

The elation they both felt showed in their first dance, the Charleston. The few observers in the theater watching the practice clapped enthusiastically when they completed the routine.

"Kate," Marco exclaimed, placing a hand on her shoulder. "You are in great form today. I almost couldn't keep up with you on the quick steps."

She laughed and shrugged, taking a drink of water from the bottle she brought with her from the room. "I was trying to keep up with you. I wasn't sure if my knees would hold up until the end. I see now why all the young ladies during the flapper era were skinny. This is work!"

Once they had a chance to catch their breath, they were ready to begin the tango routine. After the initial steps, Kate noticed Marco seemed to hold her a little closer than usual. He gazed directly into her eyes with a look that could almost be described as sad or sentimental. It felt odd, since earlier he had been so upbeat about the upcoming meeting and the prospects of everything moving on schedule with Bettina's treatments. She pushed the thoughts from her mind to focus her concentration on the dance moves.

He led her through the dramatic dance, gently holding her in the crook of his arm as he led her around the floor in a curved pattern. Their bodies moved in perfect synchronization with the intertwined staccato steps. When the music stopped, he continued to hold Kate close to him for a few seconds before suddenly backing off, mumbling something about it being almost time for dinner. They changed out of their dance shoes and quietly left the theater to head to the dining room.

It was another wonderful dinner with everyone excitedly discussing the next day's excursions. After dessert and a cup of tea, Kate bade everyone goodnight, explaining that she wanted to get a good night's sleep to be ready for the tour.

In her room, she changed into her pajamas and climbed into bed. Tomorrow would be an interesting day. She was anxious to explore cities that existed at the time pirates roamed the sea. This would be the perfect opportunity to experience some of the way of life that existed during the time period she used in her books—the time when Edward lived.

Aside from being good fodder for her books, she loved the islands. On previous visits, she always felt like she belonged there. A few years ago, she had even considered moving to one of the islands, but she knew she could never leave her family. She treasured the time she spent with Ellie and was happy her new job would keep her in Austin. She would remain close enough that they could still have their visits.

Kate readied for bed, rushing through her nighttime routine in anticipation of how nice the bed would feel on her aching muscles. As she climbed onto the soft mattress, she tried to convince herself that it was time to quit thinking and get some rest. However, her mind quickly returned to the strange look in Marco's eyes this afternoon during rehearsal. She wondered if everything was really going well or if the situation was not quite as good as he had said.

The next morning, Kate woke to the sound of the boat docking at the port of Cartagena. She quickly got out of bed to get a first look at the city. She knew the area had a very large and busy port but was surprised to see hundreds of containers lining the adjacent docks, with large cranes lifting them off the ships and onto waiting trucks. The busy port looked even larger than she remembered. She quickly showered and dressed, ready for the busy day that was planned.

Although Ellie was originally going to stick with Kate, she and Adam booked themselves a party bus tour. Kate would stick to the original excursion they planned, which also had space for the rest of the dinner group, except for Marco and Bettina, to join. Kate and her friends would set sail on a boat tour of the old forts located in the outermost bay of Cartagena. After the boat excursion, the tour would then go by bus to explore the largest Spanish fort in the New World—the Fort of San Felipe de Barajas, located in the walled old city of Cartagena. Kate was especially excited since the city had a history of pirate and privateer activity during the seventeenth and eighteenth centuries. The area offered the realism of an earlier time and would enable her to get a better feel for how the people lived their daily lives. And knowing David, she was sure she would get some good information about the deeper history of the area.

The fort itself was an impressive work of engineering. After being built, the city was afforded safety and the ability to prosper. The tour also included a stop at a shopping mall, with many shops selling Colombia's famous and exquisite jewelry. Afterwards, the foursome had agreed on a hop-on, hop-off bus tour in the modern area of Cartagena. All in all, they had an interesting and extensive tour day planned.

Leaving the cabin, Kate and Ellie headed up to the lido deck for a light breakfast and to meet up with their companions. Marco was already on his way to the meeting in town. Kate said a silent prayer that all would go well for him. As they entered the food area, she waved to Amanda who sat at a large table. Kate and Ellie decided on a bagel and some fruit. They stopped by the coffee bar then headed over to the table just as Oscar, Adam, and David walked up.

Everyone seemed excited about the day's activities. Just as Kate suspected, David had read up on Cartagena de Indias and discovered that the city was the undisputed queen of the Caribbean, a beautiful, historic township lying within the well-preserved centuries-old colonial stonewalls. David shared details of what he'd learned as the group scarfed down their breakfasts, ready to get off the ship and start the tours.

When they cleared the ship's exit area, they noticed that the staging area for shore excursions wasn't visible. The ship was tied up at a long concrete pier that seemed to stretch for miles toward a busy street lined with waiting buses and horse carriages.

Kate started laughing. "Now I understand why every shore excursion in Cartagena is listed as strenuous. I couldn't understand why taking a horse and carriage tour through the city would be listed as difficult. It's not the tour that's difficult; it's the distance passengers have to walk to get to the transportation."

Oscar grinned and nudged her with his elbow. "You mean you think walking a mile in ninety-degree heat with 100% humidity is enough to be listed as strenuous? I thought as a true Texan, you would be used to this."

"Only the Texans who live along the coast are used to this type of weather. The high humidity there used to qualify out-of-state oil workers for hardship pay when they were sent on temporary assignment anywhere on the Gulf Coast in the summer. The humidity is great for the skin but wreaks havoc on hair," she said.

Looking ahead, she called to Ellie and Adam, who were walking in front of the group. "Hey, you two, one word of caution. While you're out there enjoying your four-hour party bus tour complete with music and drinks, remember you have to make the walk again to get back to the ship in the afternoon. There'll be no carrying anyone down this pier."

"Grandma, you told me you would always be there to pick me up if I fell." Ellie teased. "What happened?"

"That was when you were around six years old and weighed about forty pounds. Now you're five foot seven and weigh around—"

"Grandma!"

Kate laughed and winked at Ellie. "Okay, we don't need to discuss weight at this time. I plan on pigging out while we're on the tour and you can too. You could stand to put on a couple of pounds."

Ellie made a face and ran ahead to catch up with Adam.

After what seemed like an interminable length of time, the group finally reached the tour staging area. Ellie and Adam left to find their brightly painted pink open bus. A tourist representative showed the rest of them to their more sedate transportation for the short ride to the boat launch, where they would board a fast boat to take them to the outer forts of San Jose and San Fernando de Bocachica in the Bay of Cartagena. The two seventeenth-century forts helped guard the city of Cartagena and were instrumental in reducing the number of attacks by pirates and privateers. The waters of the Boca Grande Channel were slightly rough as their tour boat headed towards the bay and the first fort—Fort San Jose.

Kate pulled her camera out of her travel tote and began taking pictures as she turned to David and pointed out the large stone fortress that jutted out into the bay. A long, raised concrete platform had openings underneath for seven cannons on each side of the fort, referred to as a "water flower" by the early designer of the fort.

"I really don't understand how they moved all the materials needed to build such large fortresses," David commented. "These were built in the early 1600s after Francis Drake looted and burned the city. It looks like all the stone used in construction had to be brought over by ships. Quite a feat for that time."

As their tour boat sped over to the bastion on the other side of the channel, it was obvious that any ship caught between the two fortresses would face devastating firepower from cannons pointed directly at them from both sides of the channel. Kate felt a little chill as she realized Edward could have been one of those ships. He could have faced destruction.

Oscar called to them from across the aisle. "You know, I read that along with the cannons, there were also lines and nets placed in the water that stretched from one fort to the other. Ships would get caught up in the nets and have to slow down to try and get free of the restraints. It would have been like shooting ducks in a pond."

The chill Kate had felt a moment ago came back after hearing Oscar's information. Even though she knew Edward didn't really exist, the thought of cannons and other dangers still made her feel a little troubled. Their boat circled the area around both forts and the buildings showed the ravages of time. Even though they were well maintained, they were both visible reminders of the dangers the people faced.

She quietly reflected on society during Edward's lifetime as the boat reached the dock and the group boarded the bus to head to the walled part of the city. Traffic was very heavy, since many other tourist and party buses were headed to the same place. As their bus stopped at a red light, one of the open pink buses pulled alongside the window where Kate was sitting. It was obvious the bus had been out long enough for the passengers to imbibe in a lot of the fruity Lulada Mai Tai cocktails popular in Cartagena. She stared at the bus and furrowed her brows, squinting as she tried to get a better look at one of the passengers. "Is that Marco?"

David, Oscar, and Amanda all turned to look at a tall and obviously drunk older man, wearing a panama hat with a bright pink floral hatband adorned with an equally bright pink feather. He had on a loud Hawaiian print shirt and was standing in the aisle of the bus singing and dancing the Macarena to the delight of his equally drunk bus companions.

"I really can't see his face with the sunglasses and hat," Kate pressed her face to the glass, but still couldn't get a good look. "It sure does look like Marco. And the woman sitting in the seat next to him looks like Bettina, but with brassy, blonde hair."

Before anyone could get a really good look, the buses began to move. The man quickly sat down and took his hat off to wipe the perspiration from his bald head. All four of them laughed. "That can't be Marco unless he shaved his head," David said.

Kate felt a sense of relief when she discovered it wasn't Marco after all. She hadn't been on a roller coaster in years, but her stomach had that same dropping feeling it did when she made it through the big, scary drop.

"We'll have to let him know he has a Colombian double, who also likes to dance," Oscar chimed in. "Wherever that poor guy is going, he's really going to regret his partying if he's from a cruise ship and has to walk down that long pier to get back."

They all laughed. Soon their bus left the party bus behind as they drove into the old city.

Reaching the walled city, the tour stopped near the Clock Tower at the Old City Gate. Passengers had two hours to spend walking around the city, taking pictures, shopping, or just relaxing with a good cup of Colombian coffee while engaging in the sport of people watching. As the four entered the square, Kate was surprised at the beauty. Most of the old buildings had been painted a bright yellow, including the Clock Tower. "I read in a brochure that because of its port location, this city was very important to Spain. It was easier for Spain to ship the pilfered Peruvian silver back to their country from Cartagena. Pedro de Heredia brought three ships to the Bay of Cartagena and fought a full-day battle to capture the land and establish the city. He supposedly used an indigenous woman guide, India Catalina, who helped in the Spanish conquest of Colombia by acting as an interpreter and intermediary. Supposedly, Heredia explored the area and then returned to Spain with some of the riches he acquired during his exploration, one that was rumored to be a solid gold porcupine weighing 132 pounds."

"Maybe we should head to the hills and see if we can find any of that gold," Oscar joked. "I wouldn't need to find a 132-pound armadillo, just a small five- or six-pound cat would be fine with me."

Amanda laughed and playfully hit his arm. "How do you expect to find gold hidden in the hills when you can't even find your glasses when they're right on your head?"

"Well, there is that. But if you were by my side, I'm sure you would have no problem telling me what to do."

Oscar and Amanda laughed, and the group continued walking to a narrow street across from the Clock Tower named El Portal de los Dulces, or Sweets Street. The street was lined with booths and carts selling the local favorites—coconut and panela cookies, guava jellies, and dulce de leche shaped like hearts or coins. The vendors were primarily women and eagerly offered samples of their specialties to entice the tourists.

"These would make good souvenirs to take back home. The only problem is that they would probably be gone before I ever made it there." Kate laughed then took a bite of a delicious coconut cookie.

"Then, we'll just have to buy some for ourselves and not worry about the ones we left at home." David winked at her. He purchased a handful of sweets from the vendors then offered her one to enjoy.

Kate eagerly accepted the dulces and thought about how much fun she had with the group. David was attentive and kind, Oscar always had something witty to say, and Amanda was fun and upbeat. A good mix of people.

After their purchases, the group continued the tour, passing by the house of the late Gabriel Garcia Marquez. David explained that Marquez was the Nobel Prize winning author of *Love in the Time of Cholera*. Amanda laughed at the title, saying she would have more pressing things on her mind than love during a cholera epidemic. After seeing many other beautiful buildings, the tour stopped at one of Colombia's craft beer bars. Kate and Amanda agreed that the city was wonderful, but the heat made this stop one of their favorites.

The conversation flowed freely with everyone discussing all the sights and new things they had seen.

"That guy doing the Macarena on the tour bus we saw ought to be in pretty bad shape by this time." Oscar took a sip of his cool beer and leaned back.

David laughed. "If he's on a cruise, he'll never make it back to the ship without help. I feel sorry for his wife, but she looked like this might be pretty normal for him. I just can't get over how much he reminded me of Marco. Well, until he took his hat off. Can you imagine our quiet, refined table-mate dancing on a tour bus?"

Kate looked down as she took a drink, but the hoppy liquid did little to erase the feeling of uncertainty she'd had since seeing the Marco double.

"Hey, maybe everyone has an alter ego, and we just happened to find Marco's in Colombia," Amanda joked.

David looked at his watch and stood up. "Time to get back to the tour bus."

As the group wended their way back to the bus, they continued to marvel at the beauty of the Walled City and the friendliness of the people they had encountered. Once aboard the bus, the tour continued to Santa Catalina's bastion, where they climbed up a ramp to view the watchtower and the cannons. Seeing the cannons again made Kate think of Edward. She felt the same apprehension for his safety as she had earlier in the day when they were touring the two forts.

This is insane. Edward is not real. He is a character in a book.

Though she tried, she couldn't shake the feeling that somehow Edward had been in those waters and had been subjected to the dangers that surrounded the city due to the privateers and other, more dangerous pirates.

When the bus reached the modern part of the city, Bocagrande, they had a thirty-minute stop at a shopping mall, where they could find Colombia's most famous native gem, the emerald. Amanda and Kate left to go shop while the men relaxed in a coffee bar. The emeralds were more beautiful than Kate had imagined. In no time, she found a ring she had to have. Amanda found one equally as stunning. After their purchases, they joined the men for a quick cup of coffee before rejoining the tour.

Their bus was waiting where they had been dropped off. Soon, everyone was on board ready to go back to the ship. Like everyone else, Kate wasn't ready for the long walk down the pier.

A couple of minutes into their thirty-minute ride, David leaned over to Kate. "Feel free to lean your head on my shoulder if you want to get a little rest."

Kate smiled, warmed by his kind gesture. "That's very chivalrous of you, but unnecessary."

"I'm serious, Kate. It's no problem. That pier is no joke. A little rest might help after such a long tour."

"Well, if you're sure."

He smiled and nodded. "I'm sure."

She let her head fall onto his shoulder and sighed, falling asleep almost immediately.

Back on board the ship, the group headed to the lido deck for a late snack before everyone went to their cabins to rest.

Thanks to David's offer, Kate was able to nap on the bus and could focus the rest of her afternoon on getting some writing done before meeting Marco for their dance practice.

Sitting at the keyboard, her thoughts returned to Edward and what he must have had to face every day. She hoped he would come to her soon, as there was so much she wanted to say to him, so many questions she wanted to ask. Realizing she was again letting her imagination carry her away a little too far, Kate sat up straighter in her chair and began reviewing the pictures she had taken. Pulling out her research notebook, she made notes on the various places she had seen and interesting tidbits she could use in the story. The native Colombian emeralds would be a nice addition to the treasure onboard the *Santa Magdalena*.

After an hour of reviewing pictures and setting her mind into the old, pirate world, she began typing.

Chapter Eleven

THE FIERY PASSION OF A THOUSAND BURNING SUNS

Edward

The big ship cut through the water in the calm Caribbean Sea on its course to the Atlantic Ocean. As they left his home island, Edward watched the shore growing more distant, his heart already aching to be back on his sand. He spent more of his life at sea than at home, but he always cherished the time he was able to spend relaxing on his private oasis. The thought of returning to London and seeing his brother again, though, filled him with joy enough to bid a bittersweet goodbye to his home. Norman's two boys had likely grown remarkably these past two months, and they recently added a new baby sister Edward had yet to meet.

Secretly, Edward dreamed of having a wife and family someday. He hoped to have a son he could teach, one who would be a good sailor. A child who could sail the seas with him. His life as a raider of ships would someday come to an end, though he feared for what the people he worked so hard to help would do without him. The colonization of the islands had worked in favor of the countries that took them over and less in favor of the indigenous peoples who lived there. The situation had only worsened as people from Africa were sold to the highest bidder and sent to the islands as slaves to work on the sugar plantations.

In his travels in the Caribbean, Edward had seen firsthand the deplorable conditions of the island people. Despite the riches of silver, jewels, and other natural resources that made the area profitable, the people who lived there led extremely impoverished lives. It was obvious they were being robbed by the very countries that colonized them. They did not receive the benefits of the rich resources as their rightful owners.

As he contemplated the social issues in the islands, the woman he was starting to grow attached to came up on deck. He still didn't know her name, but his heart always gave a little jump when he saw her. Her beauty shone like the setting sun, and her loving ways made her an ideal companion. She was different from the other girls he had known. The feelings he had for her grew day by day.

"Edward," she said. "I wondered where you had gotten off to."

"I be here just enjoying the sea. How be your friend? I know she be happy to return to London and see her family again, royal or not. Will ye be glad to go home too?" Edward debated not asking the last question. He feared that his woman would still run the first chance she got once they returned to safer shores.

But he needn't have worried. Her response sent his heart fluttering once more. "I haven't missed my home that much since being here on the boat with you has been wonderfully exciting. I understand your love of the sea. It is a challenging but rewarding life. You said you would be taking supplies back to the islanders when you leave. Is that still the plan?"

"Aye, that be correct. With the cargo we be saving from the Santa Magdelena, we be able to pay for needed supplies. Me brother will see that the Falcon has the goods the people need."

"Why don't you just give the money to the island's governors and let them do the work of getting things shipped?"

Edward ran a hand through his hair, shrugging at what she must have thought to be a simple suggestion. "That could be difficult since most governors might be more in favor of lining their pockets with the newfound riches than in buying supplies for a people they be thinking are inferior. No, it be better if we take everything and make sure it be given to the proper people."

"You're a good man, Edward. I know the islanders and the slaves are happy you are around. Their lives would be horribly affected if you stopped sailing and returned permanently to London."

"It be taking a strong wind to blow me off the sea." Though he treasured the time on his home island, he knew in his heart he could never fully give up the sea; she had always been his true love.

He smiled down at the woman beside him and thought perhaps the sea was not his true love after all—just his first love.

"I know that someday there be a life for me without any of the fighting that we be doing now, but I cannae imagine it not still be on a ship."

His woman smiled at him, ducking her head while lifting her eyes to meet his. "Might that life include a woman beside you?"

"I be hoping that there will be." He looked out to sea, far past the horizon, searching for answers to questions he could not voice.

She placed her hand on his. "When will that 'someday' be?"

"I not be knowing that, sweet girl. The time of someday be not up to me."

Chapter Twelve

"Grandma, are you here?" Once again, her granddaughter interrupted her writing session. Not that Kate could be too upset by it. There was a lot to think about with Edward's last thoughts.

"I'm on the balcony, Elle. Did you have a good tour?" She closed the laptop, not ready to write any more anyway.

Ellie collapsed in the adjacent chair on the balcony. "It was great, but that walk down the pier was even harder coming back than it was when we went this morning. I told Adam he might have to carry me piggyback." She laughed and stretched her legs out in front of her. "We saw one couple, probably in their sixties, really having a problem. I think the man might have had too much partying on the bus he was on. He was in bad shape. The funny thing was that when I glanced over, for a split second, I thought he looked like Marco. But he took his hat off to fan himself, and I could tell from his bald head that he wasn't."

"That is the same man we saw dancing in the aisle on one of the pink party buses we passed in the city. I had the same impression until he removed his hat. We all figured out that Marco must have an alter ego and the two lives converged here in Colombia. Was the man you saw heading to our ship or the one next to us?"

"I'm not sure. We passed them, so I didn't see which ship they got on." Ellie stood and pecked a kiss on her grandmother's cheek. "I'm tired. Think I'll take a little nap before dinner. Are you okay without my company?"

"Of course, I'm just adding notes to the book from some of the things we saw today. By the way, I bought you a little something today, but I'll wait until dinner to give it to you."

"Oh, thanks." Ellie feigned sarcasm. "Now I'll never get to sleep wondering what it is."

"I think you'll be okay. I'll be leaving to meet Marco for dance practice in a little while. In case you get up and find I'm not here, rest assured that I didn't fall overboard."

"That makes me feel better. See you later." Ellie left the balcony to go to her room.

Just as the door closed, the phone in their shared living space rang. Kate stood from the balcony chair and quickly stepped inside to answer it.

"Kate, this is Bettina. Marco wanted me to call you and let you know that his meeting is going longer than expected. He won't be able to meet you for practice today. We'll see everyone at dinner though." Bettina sounded tired, and Kate hoped she was feeling okay.

"That's fine," she replied, though she felt her heart sink a little at the news. "Tell Marco not to worry, and we look forward to seeing both of you later."

As Kate hung up the phone, she looked at her watch and saw that it was almost three. The ship was scheduled to sail at six. Marco was cutting it a little close if he was still in his meeting.

She thought about returning to her writing, but as she read over the scene she'd just written, she found herself stumped. Sometimes when she hit a little writer's block, it helped to have a cup of tea. She made herself a small cup with the electric kettle in her room and went to sit out on the balcony once more.

The view of the sea and the rhythm of the waves lulled her into a quiet, contemplative mood. She hugged the tea mug close to her chest, reveling in the warmth as she took a few sips.

She could understand why Edward loved the sea so much. It truly felt like a second home to her. The first time Kate went on a cruise, she fell in love. Living in Texas afforded her the opportunity to only drive a few hours to reach the Gulf of Mexico, which she took advantage of as often as she could. She frequently thought about purchasing a vacation home by the ocean, maybe in an area with nicer waters, like Corpus Christi or Port Aransas. But she'd watched so many of her friends' homes destroyed by hurricane after hurricane and wasn't sure if it would be worth the investment.

Looking out at the ocean now, Kate thought it just might be. What was life without a little risk?

Boring. That's what Edward would say. She could imagine him saying, *Katie girl, if you don't try, how can you know what yer missin' in life?*

She could say the same thing to him right now, she supposed. After all his whining about settling down with one woman, he sure seemed to be headed in that direction now. Millie had captured his heart—which Kate reminded herself was the whole point, though it stung a little to be edged out of her place as the most important woman in Edward's life. His assurances to her were sweet but did little to calm the aching in her heart as he fell more in love with Millie.

Kate's thoughts drifted from one man in her life to another. While Edward was quickly turning all his attention to Millie, there was another man who was turning all his attention on Kate.

The news of Marco's meeting running long could be good or bad. Either the meeting was going so well that they were doing negotiations and drawing up contracts right then, or it was going so poorly that Marco had to draw it out and keep trying to secure the investment.

Kate deeply hoped it was the former. She'd only known Marco for a matter of days, but he was kind and considerate and gentle. The way he took care of his sister touched Kate, reminding her of the protection she once had through the love of her own brothers. When they danced, Marco never made her feel foolish or inferior. He always smiled and said, "Shall we try again?"

Marco's unwavering support for Kate gave her a feeling of security she hadn't felt in years. Not only did he cure her loneliness, but he reminded her what it felt like to be cared for by a man again. To be touched, and held, and comforted. With Marco, she felt like a leading woman in his life, no longer just a sidekick in the lives of others. She started as just his dance partner, but it felt as if it could turn into something more.

As she thought about the warmth and comfort she felt with Marco, the inspiration to write came back to her. With one last look at the ocean, she headed inside and sat at her computer again, ready to work.

The time passed quickly, and soon, it was time to get ready for dinner. Kate waited in the shared sitting room for Ellie to finish getting ready. When she appeared, Kate took a small package out of her handbag and gave it to her granddaughter.

"What's this?" Ellie turned the package over in her hands.

"It's just a little something I picked up for you as a remembrance of this cruise."

She opened the box and squealed loudly when she saw the beautiful emerald ring her grandmother had given her. "Grandma, you didn't have to do this. There's no way I could ever forget this cruise. Oh my gosh! This ring is absolutely gorgeous. It fits perfectly. Thank you so much! You're the best grandma in the world. I would say that even if you hadn't gotten me a ring, but I'm really glad you did!"

The kiss on the cheek and tight hug brought tears to Kate's eyes. She always got teary-eyed when her grandchildren were close to her. The pangs of loneliness she felt from not having a love partner all these years always dissipated when she was with them.

They made their way to the dining room and found David sitting alone at the table. He stood and held Kate's chair out for her. She smiled and thanked him, grateful for such a gallant gesture from her friend. If nothing else, this cruise had gifted her with new men in her life that reminded her what it was like to be noticed as a woman.

After they settled into their seats and ordered wine, Oscar, Amanda, and Adam arrived. A few minutes later, Marco and Bettina made their way to the table. Marco looked a little pale and tired. Perhaps after such a long business meeting, the walk down the pier in the heat had been too much for him. The waiter brought everyone fried oysters as an appetizer, the chef's specialty.

"Would you like one?" Kate had never seen Marco refuse to eat, but he leaned back in his chair as if he couldn't get far enough away from the delicious fare.

"No, thank you. They look delicious, but I had a late lunch." If anything, Marco seemed paler than before. "A sad fact, as oysters are my favorite."

"Marco, we found your twin today." David speared an oyster and popped it in his mouth.

Marco looked puzzled. "My twin? I don't understand."

"One of the party buses pulled alongside our tour bus, and we saw a man who looked just like you standing in the aisle. We started to holler at him, but when he took off his hat, his bald head told us we were mistaken. With his hat on, he could be your double."

"With the meeting I was in today, I would really have rather been in the aisle of a party tour bus, singing and dancing the 'Macarena.'" Marco smiled, though it seemed forced.

The group fell silent. "You must be a mind reader. How did you know he was dancing the 'Macarena'?" David asked, head cocked to the side. Kate almost asked the same thing so waited with the rest of the group for Marco's reply.

Marco furrowed his brows, looking around the table. "I thought you had mentioned that."

Bettina's forced laughter did little to dispel the tension. "Marco, I think you are a little tired. You told me earlier that when you and your business associates went to lunch, you saw one of the party buses. They had explained that the guides on the buses usually picked the drunkest person to stand up and dance the 'Macarena.' You mentioned it must be rather common in this city."

Marco laughed. "That's right. I must have been thinking of that."

David glanced at Oscar with a questioning frown and took a drink of his Scotch. For a brief moment, Kate wondered if the man they saw really was Marco, especially with his cancellation of their dance rehearsal and how he reacted to the oysters. But she shook the thought from her head as she looked at Marco and his obviously full head of hair. Kate herself was feeling a little tired after her big day, so she couldn't blame him for feeling the same.

Adam smiled and nudged his shoulder against Ellie's. "Hey, we must have been on the wrong bus or had a new guide. No one on our bus stood in the aisle or did anything. We should ask for a refund, since we didn't get a floor show."

"Hey, I can dance for you right now if you want a show." Oscar shimmied in his seat, hands snapping in the air. "Your old man still has a few moves he can make."

Adam cringed and waved a hand at his dad. "That's okay, Pops. We'll just let it slide for now."

Everyone laughed, and the conversation shifted to the various places they had visited. Marco's doppelganger was soon forgotten as everyone recounted the day they'd had. And yet, every time plates were brought out, Marco passed. He insisted he was fine, but Kate could tell he did not feel very well. She wondered if maybe he got food poisoning from the lunch he'd had with his business associates.

As the waiter was taking orders for dessert, Marco and Bettina stood.

"We are tired after today, but we will see you in the morning for the Panama Canal. Kate, I do apologize for missing our dance rehearsal, but I will be back in form and ready to rehearse tomorrow." Beads of sweat broke out on Marco's face as he stood. Kate hoped he wasn't terribly sick.

"That's okay, Marco. I hope you feel better." She placed a hand on his forearm where he stood next to her.

"Maybe you and Kate could do the 'Macarena' as one of your dances. Evidently that's a popular dance in Central America." David raised his eyebrows at Marco.

There was an awkward beat of silence before Marco forced a smile again and said, "I think we'll just stay with the ones we have chosen. I'm not sure I'm the 'Macarena' type. Good night, everyone. See you on deck tomorrow morning." He waved goodbye, then walked arm in arm with Bettina as they wove their way out of the dining room.

The conversation turned to talk about the upcoming Panama adventure. Kate recounted her first sailing through the canal ten years earlier and how she saw the construction of the new set of locks. "It was amazing to see so many huge trucks lined up to carry the dirt away from the site. I have never seen tires that big on any vehicle. Just the tires alone had to be at least twenty feet tall. I don't know how the drivers managed to climb into the truck."

"They must have used those big Caterpillar mining dump trucks," Oscar said.

"I don't know what type they were, but I do know that they were enormous. It probably only took a couple of loads to remove all the dirt that was dug out," Kate said.

"I read that there is a new bridge over the canal," David added. "That should be a sight to see."

"I heard that too, Professor Mitchell," Adam said. Kate smiled at the young man's deference to David's professional position. It was nice to see he had manners, especially considering the way he and Ellie seemed to get along. "It's called the Centennial Bridge, and it's now a part of the Pan-American Highway. We learned that in the lecture Ellie and I attended the other day."

"I am so excited to actually get to see the canal." Amanda's grin quickly turned into a yawn. "In fact, I'm so excited that I think it is time to turn in so we can be well-rested for tomorrow."

As Amanda and Oscar rose to leave, Ellie and Adam said they were going to play video games for a little while.

David looked at Kate. "Would you like to go with me up on deck to view the planets and constellations that are visible? I can give you an idea of how ancient navigators were able to plot their course without modern navigation aids. Of course, I don't have an astrolabe or a Hadley's quadrant with me, but I can show you some of the directional stars."

"Even if you had the astro-thingamajig or the Hadley's quadrant, I wouldn't have the slightest idea what either was. I'm a total neophyte when it comes to astronomy. I studied a little since one of my characters is a navigator on the pirate ship, but my knowledge is still limited. I would love to know more about how a ship could know where it was during any given time."

They headed to the promenade deck, walking closely as he led her to an unlit seating area that gave a wonderful view of the night sky. Rather than sitting down at one of the small tables, they went to stand at the railing, looking out at the sea while they waited for their eyes to adjust to the dark.

She turned towards David. "Thank you so much for your company on the various tours we have taken. It has been nice to have someone to share and discuss all the wonders we have seen. I hope we can remain friends after we return home."

"I'd like that very much, Kate. It has been good to have someone to talk with again and just feel the physical presence of another human being." He sighed and looked up at the night sky. "I've been pretty much locked up emotionally since the death of my wife." He paused after this confession. Kate gave him space in the silence, allowing him to gather his thoughts and steer the conversation. After a moment, he turned to her and smiled. "I didn't realize how much I've missed socializing until we all became friends. I think I'm a little sorry that Marco asked you to dance before I had a chance. I'm still a little hesitant to get back in the game again, I think. My well-intentioned friends are constantly inviting me over to dinner, and there usually happens to be an extra woman at the table. They really don't understand subtlety."

"Oh, I know what you mean." Kate turned her body to lean sideways against the railing, facing David more fully. "My friends are always contriving ways to pair me up with numerous available men, who are very nice, but I just am not into blind dates. Maybe it's age, but the dating game just doesn't appeal to me. I want to meet someone on my own and form a friendship first, then see what happens from there. I guess I really want no pressure pairing. Just me and a man, forming a connection. In today's society, I don't know if that is a real thing or not anymore."

"I think it is. People need to relax and not get frantic trying to find Mr. or Miss 'Right.' My motto is let life happen and appreciate what you have."

"That's a great philosophy. Very refreshing to hear. Do you have children?"

At the mention of children, David's face lit up. "Yes. I have a son, David Junior, who is with the diplomatic service and is assigned to the US Embassy in England. He and his wife live in London with my two grandchildren—Elizabeth, who's almost twenty-one, and Albert, who's twenty-three. We get together once a year, but Skype frequently enough that I can keep up with all the family happenings. The grandkids want to come spend a summer with me one of these years. I can't wait. Albert is considering grad school here in the US and wants to check out the University of Texas' programs." David practically gushed as he spoke of his family. Despite his love for academics, Kate had never seen him more animated than when he shared his son's and his grandchildren's accomplishments.

"That would be exciting. They are close in age to Ellie and Adam. Hopefully, you and I will remain friends, and when your grandkids come, we can all spend some time together." She smiled and squeezed his arm before letting go and turning back to the railing. She gazed up at the sky. "Now I want to spend some time with the stars."

David stood quietly beside her for several minutes then leaned over and pointed out a constellation midway up in the sky. "Kate, look a little to the left and up just a little bit. Do you see a bright star?"

Kate squinted up in the direction he pointed. She thought the stars might be hard to make out on a moving ship, but they were easy to see. Despite the boat's rocking, the stars were a steady presence in the night sky. "I think so. Is that it up there?"

"Yes. That is Ursa Minor, usually referred to as the Little Dipper. The bright star at the end of the dipper handle is Polaris. That star points due north. If a navigator knew which way was north, then it was easy to determine the other directions. Navigators in the middle and late eighteenth century had the new quadrant, which they could use to find the latitude by measuring the angular height above the horizon. But they also needed to measure longitude, and that was more difficult. Having the accurate time was extremely important since fifteen degrees of longitude corresponds to one hour of time difference. Accurate instruments were needed to measure the distance of the moon and nearby stars. The needs of ancient navigators were responsible for the establishment of observatories like the one in Greenwich. An accurate time measuring instrument was developed in 1764 and—"

Kate interrupted him and started laughing. "David, I'm

not sure I totally understand everything you've said, but my brain is about to explode. I'm sure that all of the ancient navigators had to be mathematical geniuses to be able to figure out a ship's location. I can see what you are saying about the position of the planets and stars, but what on earth happened when there was a storm or a period of cloudy nights where no stars could be seen?"

"Bad weather was a navigator's worst enemy. Without being able to take visual measurements, ships were frequently thrown miles off their route and were sometimes lost. The British Royal Navy lost a whole squadron of ships off the coast of England in the Scilly Isles. They had been sailing for days under overcast and cloudy skies, but the navigators believed they were sailing on the same latitude as France. Using that information, the admiral set a course for home. Later that night, the flagship slammed into the rocks and sank within minutes. Their ship was followed by three others. Well over one thousand men were lost at sea in just one night."

"That is terrible." Kate kept her eyes focused on the stars, trying not to imagine Edward in a situation like that. "When I look up at the stars at night, especially on a cruise ship in the middle of the ocean, I have a very difficult time comprehending the vastness of the universe and what lies beyond it."

"That is a popular discussion in science. There are theories that death is just moving into a different existence. That our life span is similar to the existence we lived while in the womb. Dying is really just being born again. There are people who believe that the fourth dimension is time;

that there are three spatial and one time coordinates. That theory produces some pretty radical ideas. Take your books for example. You write about Captain Peregrine and his environment with familiarity. You know his emotional and physical feelings. You know his world and his actions. Is he just an illusion of your imagination or have you some-how been tapping into another existence somewhere on the time-space continuum? You might also have crossed over to the spirit world and are seeing the ghost of your captain. Another theory could be that you have created an alternate universe for your captain, and through your writings, he is able to live in that world. In his case, since he is helping you with the story line, he can almost tailor-make his existence and enjoy a wonderful life. My favorite premise would be that you, through some dramatic event, merged the time-space continuum with the spirit world and are giving life to the captain through your writings. That sounds like a wild theory, but it's not out of line with some of the other the-ories floating around. The truth is, no one knows what lies beyond our universe."

Kate thought for a moment before she replied. "That sounds like something from *The Twilight Zone*. So, some people think that there could be a fold or crinkle in time, and we might overlap with an alternate universe, or that we might access the spirit world?" Kate shuddered. "That is too much for this old brain." She turned away from the railing to look at David. "I have totally enjoyed this evening. Thank you so much for enlightening me on the aspects of navigation. From what I've learned now, I know I'll never take up sailing."

David laughed. "Just remember, GPS has solved all the problems of getting from one place to another, so you can buy that boat."

"Now that's funny. My GPS has sent me on some pretty strange drives. Once, I thought I was going through someone's backyard. We even drove next to an old-fashioned clothes' line with the day's wash pinned to it. I don't know if I could trust GPS to get me anywhere in a boat."

David took her arm and walked with her to the elevators. "Kate, you are a fun and intelligent woman. We should do this again sometime. It might not be as exciting as the proverbial dancing on tables, but you have to admit that it's a little less strenuous physically." He gave her a quick hug. "I'm excited about tomorrow. You will have to explain everything to our group as we go through the locks on the canal."

Kate was surprised by his hug but was glad he felt comfortable with her since she had really enjoyed his company. "Well, I don't know if I can explain everything, but maybe I'll come up with something that even you don't know," she teased as they boarded the elevator.

Chapter Thirteen

$\mathcal{K}$ate closed the door to the suite and noticed she was alone. Ellie must still be out with Adam. Though she loved her granddaughter, Kate enjoyed the quiet time when she could reflect on the day. The tour had been enjoyable, but so had the time David took to show her the stars and explain how ships navigated in years past. She was excited to tell Edward everything she had seen and learned about his world today. She also wanted to warn him about the dangers of the forts in the waters around Cartagena.

She opened the mini fridge and took out the bottle of wine she had ordered. She poured a small amount into a glass and walked out to the balcony. Even at night, the water was exciting. The ship parted the seaway, creating foamy white waves that shattered against the steel hull. She had always loved the sounds of the sea and leaned back in her chair to let her mind process the journey thus far.

Marco was first in her thoughts. He had opened her up to a world of fun and excitement. He was always so positive and supportive, even with all the problems he had in his life. She could have never imagined she would be participating in a dance contest and actually enjoying it. He made her feel young and attractive again.

Oscar and Amanda were wonderful company—upbeat, adventurous, and always laughing. Kate hoped they would continue their friendship after the cruise was over.

Then, there was David. When she thought of the men in her life earlier, she had not considered David. Now, after the night they'd had, she couldn't help but add him to the mix.

David was quiet and studious, but his eyes always held a twinkle. He was an easy person to be around. Though he had not mentioned it before tonight, Kate had figured out that he was a widower during some of their earlier conversations. When men lose their spouse after years of marriage, they had an air of loneliness and loss about them. It was like looking at a single shoe. On the surface, it looks fine, but it needs a mate to be complete. She smiled as she thought how much David was like an older Edward, not just in looks, but also in actions and feelings. She was comfortable with David and found his knowledge a desirable trait, one she was happy he was willing to share.

She had been on cruises before, but this one really stood out as one of the better ones she had taken. Ellie probably would agree with her. Adam was turning out to be someone who would be a fixture in Ellie's life even after the boat docked in Galveston.

The wine plus the pleasant thoughts and happy feelings relaxed Kate. She headed back inside to get a good night's sleep.

～◌～

"Kate, ye be asleep?"

Kate had just drifted off when she heard Edward's voice. "Edward! I was hoping you would visit soon. I have so much to tell you."

He smiled as he took a seat on the side of the bed. "Ye look like ye be having a good time. I see in ye the beauty of a happy woman. What has caused ye to feel the excitement of life?"

"Edward, it was wonderful." She sat up, making sure to keep the blanket tucked under her arms. "We went to Cartagena and took a boat tour of the two forts guarding the entrance to the channel leading into the old city. It was scary to see the forts standing just opposite of each other with a whole line of cannons pointed out into the water. Then, we went into the old city and walked around. We saw the old clock tower and other places. I almost felt like I was visiting someplace you had been. I had a real sense of connection with your life. It was a wonderful tour." Kate was breathless as she described the events of the tour and all the sights.

"Aye, Kate. Cartagena is a grand place. I can't say that I enjoyed seeing the forts, but we never be having troubles there. Was Marco with ye?"

"No, he had business in town. I went with David, Oscar, and Amanda. We all got along well, and everyone was impressed with what we saw."

"That be good. David is a good man. I think the flag he flies is a true one. I be happy that ye have someone to enjoy all the beautiful views with. I think David is a better man than Marco."

The bold statement took her aback. For someone who'd never interacted with either man, Edward seemed to have a strong opinion. His assumptions irritated her. She frowned and crossed her arms. "Why do you think that? You don't even know them, and yet you have made a judgment on their characters. Marco is a fine man. He seems to be attracted to me, and that makes me feel good. I don't understand why you have to be so sanctimonious in your opinion of him."

"Kate, why do ye always take what I say in the wrong way? I not be criticizing Marco. I just think he be not what he appears."

She sat up further and leaned forward. To hear Edward voice doubts Kate didn't even realize she'd been having until now made her feel insecure and question her own ability to judge someone's character. Her eyes narrowed as she glared at Edward, and she responded in a sharp, crisp tone. "Well, I think you are wrong about him. He has done nothing but be very nice and respectful to me. I think you might just be a little jealous that I finally have someone too!"

"Jealous, is it? I'll have ye know that I not be having a jealous bone in me body. Go ahead. Be with Marco. But be warned, he is flying a false flag."

Kate rolled her eyes. "Edward, you and your false flags. You are so suspicious. I just want to have fun and be young again, even if it is only for a few more days. Don't destroy that for me, please."

He sighed and leaned forward to tenderly caress her cheek. "Kate, I only be wanting ye to be joyous and safe. Ye be a wonderful woman, but ye are a little too trusting. But, ye be right, enjoy these days. Dance and laugh all the day and night! Go to sleep, Kate, ye have a busy time coming."

Kate felt the sleep return just as Edward removed his hand from her cheek. Before leaving, she thought she felt him kiss her lightly on the forehead and whisper, "Be safe, Katie girl. I care for ye and want ye to be happy, but there be things coming that be a true worry."

~

Hours later, confusion still clouded her mind. Kate couldn't quite understand what Edward had said even in the morning's welcome light. She'd have to wait until later to question him.

She had never seen the lido deck so crowded at breakfast time. Everyone was up early and ready to begin the half crossing of the canal. She and Ellie eyed the busy room, looking for anyone from their group. Ellie spotted David standing up and waving at them from a table across the dining room. They headed over to join him.

"It looks like everyone on the ship is here," Kate exclaimed, still looking around at the crowd. "Have you seen anyone else from our group?"

"Oscar, Amanda, and Adam are getting their breakfast. I waved to Marco and Bettina when they came in, so they know where we are sitting. Why don't the two of you go ahead and get what you want? When the others get here, I'll get mine."

"Sounds good. If someone comes by with a pot of coffee, would you mind having them leave a couple of cups for Ellie and me?" Kate asked as the two walked toward the line.

They piled their plates with large helpings of eggs, bacon, grits, and toast then returned to the table where their group was already sitting, sans David. She knew he must have been off getting his own food. She looked over at Marco, who seemed a little better off than he was yesterday. Though it did look like he kept to a light breakfast of toast and grapefruit.

"It looks like the two of you have healthy appetites this morning." Amanda smiled.

"We have to keep our strength up for the busy day ahead. It takes a lot of work getting this ship through the locks, and we want to be ready for whatever the day brings." Kate joked. "Besides, it felt a little cooler this morning. We need enough calories to keep us warm."

"It did feel cooler. I think it rained during the night and that took the temperature down," Oscar added. "Panama must have noticed my hot presence arrive." Amanda rolled her eyes at her husband's joke in a way that made Kate think he probably made it frequently.

David returned to the table with his breakfast and sat in the chair next to Kate. Finishing their breakfasts, they enjoyed a second cup of coffee before walking up the stairs to the open deck on the next level. She glanced around to see what looked familiar and what had changed. Past the front of the ship, she could just see the outline of a huge bridge crossing over the canal.

"Now that's new." She pointed at the bridge for the others to see. "That must be the new Centennial Bridge. I had no idea it was that large."

The group watched as the ship slowly sailed towards the looming cable-stayed design bridge until they were close enough to cross under the main span, which was already teeming with traffic.

"I heard there are six lanes of traffic on the bridge, and that the bridge has a clearance of 262 feet," Adam said as they were directly under the span. "Looking back at the height of our stacks it looks like a tight fit, but I'm sure there's more room than it appears."

"I certainly hope so," Amanda responded.

As the ship passed slowly under the bridge, Kate could see the beginning of the new locks. Before long, tugboats would attach to their cruise ship to guide them through the entrance into the first of three locks they would go through, allowing the ship to eventually be raised eighty-five feet. Everyone bustled around taking pictures and waving at the workers next to the concrete walls of the locks. As the tugs maneuvered the large vessel into position, Kate glanced at the high walls beside them. Marco and David were leaning on the railing, trying to look down into the water to see all the activity below. Huge steel gates on each side of the passageway were beginning to slide together to make a sealed enclosure that would be flooded when the gates were completely in place.

"This is different," Kate said. "On the old locks, the ships were hooked up to locomotives, called mules, and they pulled the ship through the various locks. I also remember the steel doors swung closed instead of sliding together."

"Why did they call the locomotives mules?" Ellie asked.

Before Kate could answer, Oscar said, "I read that when the canal was first opened, they used teams of mules to pull the boats through. I don't think they could get enough mules together to pull some of the ships I've seen waiting to come through this opening."

"I've heard it costs shipping companies around five hundred thousand dollars for a ship to go through the canal. Even more if the ship is really large," Marco said.

"I guess the companies justify the cost by the time savings and reduced costs of the voyage," David responded. "It can save a ship up to three weeks in travel time by not having to go around Cape Horn."

"No wonder this cruise was so expensive," Oscar joked.

Ellie pointed out how much the ship was being raised and where the deck was now in relation to the concrete dock beside them.

Amanda just shook her head. "I'll never understand how water can lift a ship of this size. I know it has to do with the ability of the ship to float, but it just logically doesn't seem possible that it could raise something this massive."

At that point, the tugs began to push the ship towards the second lock, where the procedure started all over again. As everyone looked over the rail, one passenger pointed out a dolphin playing alongside the ship and enjoying the rising water.

Marco stood by Kate and shook his head. "This is amazing. I couldn't even imagine something like this. Does the area look very different to you, or do you still see some things that are the same?"

"Not really, with the trees, we can't see the original lock. When I crossed the first time, we were able to see all the work being done, but there really wasn't enough completed that we had an idea of what the finished project would look like."

"Well, this was definitely worth the trip."

Kate glanced at him and laid her hand over his. "I'm glad that you're feeling better and are able to enjoy this. You need something to keep your mind off of other things."

"I'll have my answer hopefully by tomorrow." Marco smiled and briefly touched her shoulder. "Today is for fun and relaxation. Plus, we get to pick up our costumes for the contest today."

"That's right!" Kate exclaimed. "I had almost forgotten. I can't wait to see what they put us in."

"I don't know about that. I might be able to wait." He laughed.

Though he seemed to be in brighter spirits today, Kate still wondered about the circumstances of yesterday. Was there any truth to what Edward said? She had always been some-one to give the benefit of the doubt, and that wouldn't stop now. She would choose to see the good in Marco until he did something outrageous to prove otherwise.

Through the morning, the group continued watching the progress of the cruise ship passing through the canal. Passengers spent the time searching for dolphins and wav-ing to the workers on the land beside the locks. After the third and last lock, the ship had been successfully raised the eighty-five feet. The tugs towed it to a location in the large Gatun Lake, where they would wait until it was time for the trip back.

Kate was amazed at the number of cargo ships and tankers lined up ready to go through the canal. As they had about a two- or three-hour wait, everyone decided it was time for food again, since they had eaten breakfast so early. After a delightful lunch of fresh salmon and salads, she sat back in her chair, smiling as she listened to the others laughing and talking around her. What a cohesive group of new friends. Everyone was so relaxed and seemed to enjoy playfully teasing each other. Even Marco and Bettina were enjoying themselves. Was Edward's seafaring life as energizing for his crew as this was for her?

The rocking motion of the ship as it started moving again brought Kate back from her musings. Everyone headed back upstairs to watch the return passage.

When the ship passed under the Centennial Bridge again, Kate and Marco left to go to the theater and choose their costumes. Casey met them as they entered the lobby.

"Kate! Marco! Over here. I've got all the costumes that are available in this room." They followed Casey to a large room in the back of the theater. Casey looked at them up and down as if she were mentally assessing their sizes before commenting. "You two are dancing a Charleston and a tango. I think I have the ideal costume for each of them."

She went to a rack and pulled out a white sleeveless, sequined dress with fringe covering the skirt from the waist down. The dress length was slightly above the knee, allowing, as Casey said, for ease of movement for the more difficult steps. She topped off the ensemble with a silver headband that held a large fluffy white feather.

Kate looked at the rather revealing dress and again was glad she had been attending Zumba classes these past few months in anticipation of the cruise. Marco's outfit consisted of a black suit, a black shirt with white suspenders, and a white silk tie. To complete his costume, Casey added black-and-white spectator shoes.

She led them to another rack. "Okay, we've got the Charleston ready. Now let's go pick out something for the tango."

Kate's eyes were immediately drawn to a red-and-black horizontal-striped long-sleeve, fitted tee and a slinky, below-the-knee black skirt with a very high side slit. A black beret, black heels, and a long cigarette holder completed the look. Marco chose fitted black slacks and a black, long-sleeve fitted man's shirt. After choosing the costumes, Casey sent each of them to a fitting room to try on their selections. Marco was already dressed in his Charleston outfit when Kate hesitantly walked out of the dressing room.

"Wow!" Casey exclaimed. "You look great."

Marco stood there staring at Kate, a smile in his eyes. "Kate, you are absolutely stunning."

"This dress is a little shorter than I realized. I don't know if a woman my age should be wearing something like this." Despite his comforting words, she still wasn't sure this was the right dress.

Raising one eyebrow, Marco looked at Kate and playfully responded, "Believe me, Kate. You could compete with any age group. That dress is perfect, and you are perfect in it."

Kate still felt a little flustered, but he walked over, took her hand, and led her to the large mirror on the wall. The mirror showed a tall, dark, and handsome man, and a lady who looked half her age in an outfit reminiscent of a flapper from an F. Scott Fitzgerald novel. Seeing herself next to Marco gave her a little more confidence to keep this costume.

"You two are going to knock them dead just walking on the stage. Try on the other costumes, and let's see what kind of effect they have." Casey clapped her hands in delight.

The second set of costumes were dramatic, a completely

different look than the Roaring Twenties. "You make a handsome couple." Casey grinned. "I can't wait to see you on the floor."

"Thank you, but we're just friends. We only met at the start of the cruise." Kate wasn't sure why she was protesting. Didn't she want a relationship with Marco? Were Edward's seeds of doubt starting to take root?

"No one would ever know that you just met. The way you dance and interact with each other, it's like watching a happily married couple enjoying their life together." Casey sighed.

Marco took Kate's hand and turned to look at the mirror's reflection of them. Smiling, he said softly, "That's exactly how I feel. We seem to have hit it off perfectly. I couldn't imagine a better dance partner, Kate."

His words reassured her a little, but the doubt remained. It had only been a little over a week. All this talk of being a couple felt like too much for such a new friendship.

"Well, you may not be a couple right now, but after you win the dance contest and accept the couples' prize, who knows what will take place? Remember the TV show *The Love Boat*? There were all kinds of romances that began with a cruise. It could happen." Casey winked and gathered up the costumes, then put them in a clothes bag with their names on the outside. "Okay, we've taken care of that. Thanks, you two. I really appreciate all you're doing to help make this show a success."

"Thank you. We've been enjoying it." Kate smiled but still felt a little ill at ease. Things were moving quickly, and she wasn't sure if the feelings she enjoyed with Marco were real or just the result of being on a relaxing vacation and the calming effect of the sea. She wondered if the situation was getting a little out of her control and after being a single woman for so many years, she was uncomfortable when she wasn't making the decisions. She pushed those thoughts aside as they left the theater.

Walking to the elevators, Kate turned to Marco. "I want you to know that I really appreciate you being my partner in the contest. This is the most exciting thing I have done in years."

Marco looked at her and smiled. "I'm glad you are enjoying the contest. You are really an outstanding dancer. For someone who had lessons only as a child, you are a wonderful dancer."

"I've always loved to dance. I even dance around the house when I'm alone. Moving to music is the most relaxed feeling in the world; though I have to admit that our Charleston routine is a little bit of a workout. I'm glad I was faithful to my exercise classes this past year."

Marco laughed. "I understand that. I, too, love to dance, but each year, it gets a little more difficult to get the quick steps down. Have a good rest of the afternoon, Kate. I'll see you at dinner in a little while."

"Thanks, Marco."

He leaned down and gently kissed her on the forehead before walking to his cabin.

Kate entered the suite. The activities of the day had really been fun and seeing the new locks at the canal was very educational. Practice went well and Marco was being so attentive to her, even with his situation. Yet instead of being deliriously happy, she was plagued with doubts. Whether she wanted them to or not, Edward's warnings had stayed with her. It was the reason why Casey's mistaken thought that she and Marco were married made her so defensive.

On the other side of the coin, Kate wondered what was going on with David. She was beginning to feel a closeness to him. Just seeing him made her smile. She leaned back on the couch and shut her eyes tightly, thinking, *I have to focus on the book now. I don't need any personal drama in my life at this time!* She stood up and headed to her bedroom to get ready for dinner.

~◯~

At dinner, she was surprised to see everyone looking so lively after the long day. The conversation centered on the half passage through the canal and what a wonder of construction it was.

As soon as everyone was seated, Amanda said, "We never realized how much fun a cruise was. This one has been great so far. The canal passage was amazing. Everything on the ship has been perfect. In fact, we are already thinking about another cruise for the coming spring."

"Where are you thinking about going?" David asked. "I've heard that an Alaskan cruise is really something to see."

Oscar nodded. "We were looking into an Alaskan cruise."

"An Alaskan cruise was my very first, and it was wonderful," Kate said. "The scenery, the whales playing, the exceptional views of snowy mountains, and the glaciers calving; everything we saw was incredible. Alaska is definitely one cruise I would like to take again some time."

Marco smiled. "Maybe we should all plan to take an Alaskan cruise together someday. This trip has certainly been enjoyable. I cannot think of better traveling companions."

Bettina nodded in agreement. "That would be fun. I have really enjoyed myself on this trip, and it's because of all of you. I want to thank you for that." She looked down as if to hide tears.

"Well," Oscar said as he stood, "I hate to leave a good party, but this has been a long day, and I'm ready for a little shut-eye."

Everyone at the table agreed, stood, and headed out of the dining room.

"We've got another big day tomorrow in Limon," David said. "Hope the weather holds out for our rainforest tour. I noticed a lot of ominous clouds forming at sundown."

"Don't worry, old man," Oscar replied as they walked. "They'll get us on that tour no matter what the weather is."

Kate was glad they were all returning to their rooms early since she planned a full schedule for the next day.

They had decided to take a bus, train, and boat tour of the area around Limon and hoped to see some of the wildlife there as well as the beautiful banana tree farms and other foliage. She had liked Costa Rica very much the last time she visited and was glad to get a chance to see more of the country. The tour didn't start until 1:00 p.m. That would give her time in the morning to get some more writing done. She had reached the part where the ship was threatened by a terrible storm, and Millie would prove her love by risking her life to help Edward. Just as Kate was thinking about the storm, she heard a loud clap of thunder outside. Light from a nearby lightning bolt reflected on the sliding door of the balcony. She smiled, thinking it must be a good omen that the weather was helping her set the stage for a pivotal part of the story.

As she climbed into bed, she wondered if Edward would visit tonight. She was so tired she was afraid she wouldn't wake if he did. The sound of the rain and the storm outside overtook her as soon as her head hit the pillow. She was lulled into a deep, restful sleep.

⟋⟍

"Kate, I do not want to wake ye tonight. Ye seem so peaceful and happy in yer sleep. There be a storm coming near, so be prepared and dinnae let anything or anyone cause ye dismay. Just be happy, Katie girl." Edward sat on the bed, looking down at Kate for a long time before he gently kissed her cheek and slowly faded away.

⟋⟍

Promptly at 6:00 a.m., Kate woke up refreshed and ready to get working. She ordered breakfast, quickly showered, and dressed in sweatpants and a matching shirt. It was still raining outside, and the day was dreary. The weather report was for the rain to move out midmorning, but the skies would still be cloudy. Since the balcony was still wet from the rain, she set up her workstation in the sitting room, knowing Ellie would probably sleep late after the long day yesterday. Just as Kate had everything ready, her breakfast arrived along with the much-needed coffee. The server put the tray on the desk. She was now ready to write.

Chapter Fourteen

THE FIERY PASSION OF A
THOUSAND BURNING SUNS

Millie

The sky was overcast, and dark clouds hovered just above the horizon. Edward and Millie stood on the deck, arm in arm, watching the rainbow-colored mist that hung over each wave as it splashed against the wooden hull of the ship. She knew their time together was shortened. Each day they drew closer to England, closer to goodbye. Edward was going to have a visit with his brother before heading back to the islands, and Lady Teresa would be returned to the loving arms of the grand duke and duchess. Millie felt a sadness wash over her that was almost stronger than she could bear.

"Captain," the helmsman called. "I think we may be heading into bad weather."

Edward walked to the wheel and looked through the glass at the dark clouds slowly overtaking the ship. The seas were beginning to churn, and the wind had picked up. He shouted to the crew to batten the hatches, run up the storm jib sail, and attach ropes to the deck that could be used for safety by anyone walking on the deck during high winds. He ordered the helmsman to keep the boat heading into the waves and all non-essential crew were sent below to safer quarters. Henry and Lady Teresa had come up on deck to see what was happening and were immediately ordered back to the cabin along with Millie.

The crew readied the ship as best they could for the approaching storm and then went below, ready to bail any water that came from the crashing waves. Millie watched through the open cabin door as the helmsman was struggling to keep the ship on course. He was in the process of lashing himself to the wheel when a strong gust of wind hit the ship, spinning the wheel hard against his arm and knocking him down to the deck. His scream of pain reached Millie's ears through the high winds and into her cabin.

Edward ran over and looked at the helmsman's limp arm, then sent him below deck with the help of another crewmember. With quick movements, Edward lashed himself to the wheel and steered the ship into the waves. From her vantage point, she could see the strain of his muscles as he fought the wind and heavy seas. She was overcome with fear that he would lose the battle and be swept overboard into the crashing waves. The thunder cracked like the loud retort of the large cannons on board. Lightning flashed in a constant barrage of bright light that devilishly danced all around them in the fury of the sea.

As Millie watched, a large menacing wall of water came over the aft deck and broke just over the wheel where Edward was. Water washed over him until he was out of sight. She screamed his name in fear, but as the water ran down the deck, she could see him still fighting at the wheel. Without thinking, she ran up the steps. Holding tightly to the ropes on the deck, she hurriedly made her way to where he stood, ready to help.

"Aye, girl! What ye be doing? Get below deck and protect yerself!" Edward barked.

Tears streamed down her cheeks. "No, Edward. I will not leave you here alone to fight this storm. I am a strong woman from years of hard work. I can help you hold the wheel."

"Ye be crazy. Ye cannae hold this wheel. The wind is too strong. Save yerself!"

"No! I will not leave you, and you can't let go of the wheel to take me back to the cabin," Millie screamed to be heard over the howling wind.

"Aye, ye be a hardheaded wench. Lash yourself to the wheel and hold on!"

She took a rope and tied herself tightly to the post supporting the wheel, then stood close to Edward and placed her hands next to his, holding the bucking wheel against the relentless force of the strong winds. They stood silently, fighting the strength of Mother Nature, and kept the boat headed into the waves. Lighting flashed beside the boat, then one bold flash struck the mast, leaving an eerie blue glowing ball of flame clinging to the top.

Looking at the flickering blue lights, Edward yelled, "Girl! Look ye there. That be St. Elmo's fire on the mast."

She looked up, fascinated but scared by the phenomenon.

"That be a good sign for us," he added.

The lights on the mast lasted only a few seconds before they faded away, yet the storm continued its relentless attack on the ship. The roar of the wind and the sound of waves crashing over the boat were deafening. Millie was afraid the masts would break, and they would flounder in the angry sea. They stood together, battling the fierce storm with the ship rising with each approaching wave and then crashing down again only to be assaulted by another. They seemed to work together as one, using their strength to hold the wheel steady. The ship groaned and creaked in complaint from the force of the strong winds and waves, but she held strong and managed to stay afloat despite the torrents of water crashing on the decks. Finally, after what seemed like mere minutes and excruciating hours all at once, the winds slowly died down. The clouds began to retreat, allowing a small glimpse of blue sky above.

"Aye, girl. Ye did a fine job." His look of admiration warmed her through her soaked clothes. As he gazed at her with pure warmth in his eyes, she knew she couldn't keep it a secret any longer. After all they'd been through and all they'd shared, he had to know who she truly was.

"Edward, I can't lie to you anymore. I am just a handmaiden. My name is Millie, and I've been with Lady Teresa for the last five years. I realized while we battled the storm that we could have been killed, and I would leave this earth with a lie on my lips. I had to tell you the truth. Do with me what you want, but at least my conscience is clear." She must look a fright with her dress clinging to her body, her hair in a tangled mess, and desperation in her eyes. But she no longer cared.

Edward reached down and brushed the wet hair away from her face. "Millie, I think I knew ye be the handmaiden. I dinnae care who ye be or what ye have done in yer life. I know that ye be the girl I fancy, and I want ye with me for as long as our time be lasting." Edward leaned down and took her in his arms. "What ye didn't know was that there be another ship waiting to come to the Santa Magdalena to capture Lady del Gado for ransom. They be not honorable men and most likely would have collected the ransom and then killed the both of ye. Once they saw that ye be on the Falcon, they went back to the open sea to find another target." Edward paused, then said, "As soon as we arrive in England, I will contact the grand duke to let him know that we have arrived and Lady Teresa be safe. Ye be free to go back with her."

Millie tightened her arms around him. "Edward, I don't want to go back. I want to stay here with you and live where you live."

"Aye, ye be sayin' that now, but a life at sea be a hard life for a young woman. Ye would soon grow tired of the hardships and want to return to civilization. There could also be dangers from other ships or even on the islands."

"That could be true, Edward, but I want to be with you. I've known hardships in my life before. I can handle myself in dangerous situations. Being with you and sailing the seas would be a dream life. You could teach me all about ships and how to sail, and when we're on your island, I could make you a home and prepare your meals just like a proper lady."

Edward smiled down at her winsome face alive with youthful exuberance. "Millie, having ye with me on the ship has been more than satisfying to me. Ye be a breath of fresh air in a sometimes difficult world. But I not be holding ye to make decisions that ye might come to regret. If ye want to stay with me for a time to see how the sea life be, I will think about what ye ask. But if I decide to let ye stay and after a time ye be unhappy, ye must tell me so arrangements can be made to send ye back home."

Millie reached up a hand to touch Edward's face. She cradled his cheek in her hand, brushing her thumb across his cheekbone. "I could never be unhappy with you."

They stared at each other for a long moment, soaking in the joy of finally being together with no secrets between them. Finally, Edward turned his head and kissed her palm. "If ye want to be with me, I be a fool to turn ye down. I think ye belong by my side, Millie."

She grinned up at him, then pressed herself against his body and squeezed tightly again. "Oh, Edward, you have made me the happiest girl in the world. I'll work hard as any man during the day, and I'll love you as a woman at night to keep you happy."

He laughed at her response and playfully slapped her on the bottom. "Come, girl. Let's go below and see what damage has been done."

As they went downstairs, they could see the crew cleaning up the water that had run down the stairs during the storm. They entered the main cabin and saw Lady Teresa and Henry standing by the seated helmsman who had a deftly applied sling on his arm. Millie could tell by Edward's face that he was puzzled by the skills it took to fasten such a sling.

"How be ye?" Edward asked.

Fernando looked towards Henry with gratitude. "It's fine, Captain. It was just a dislocated shoulder, but Henry pulled my arm and pushed it back into the socket. After that, it doesn't hurt much."

Relief flooded Edward's voice as he said, "That be good. I'll have Armando take over the wheel for a few days until ye recover. Now, go get some rest. Ye have had a difficult day."

"Aye, Captain. Thank you."

Edward turned to Henry. "I dinnae know ye knew how to doctor a man, Henry."

"I didn't either. I just found a book in your cabin and followed the instructions. I know the poor bloke must have felt a lot of pain, but he never uttered a cry."

"That be typical. We be havin' a good, strong crew. Now, I think we all be needin' a wee drop of rum to calm our nerves." Edward's long legs made short work to the cabinet on the back wall, where he produced a bottle of rum and some glasses.

They all sat around the round table, finally able to relax after their experience. Everyone gratefully took a glass of the amber liquid. The crew hoped they had survived the worst and that the next few weeks would be smooth sailing until they reached their destination. Millie smiled at the crew, thinking about what it would be like to live with them permanently, what it would be like to be a part of this family. Her eyes drifted to Edward, laughing at a joke one of his crew members told, and she sighed happily. She couldn't wait to get back to London so she could tender her resignation and begin her new seafaring life, side by side with her lover.

Kate stopped to check the time. The group was to meet at noon for a quick lunch and then head to join the tour. This was the first tour all of them would go on together. She was excited and hoped the weather would clear up just a little, though rain in the rainforest was to be expected. As she was saving her work and closing her computer, Ellie walked sleepily from her room.

"Wow! I slept like a log. What time is it?"

"It's just a little after eleven. You still have an hour to get ready for lunch. You really were a sleepy head this morning." Kate laughed.

"I know. The rain and waves just kept me relaxed and drowsy. I love being on a ship in a storm. It's so calming."

You wouldn't think that if you had experienced the storm Edward just went through.

Satisfied with the state of her book, Kate went to get ready herself. She hoped Marco and Bettina would like the tour. Since the weather was so overcast, Bettina shouldn't have any issue with the bright sun.

Chapter Fifteen

*J*ust as Kate and Ellie were ready to walk out the door, the phone rang. Kate hurried over to answer it and was surprised to hear Marco's voice.

"Kate, this is Marco. I hate to tell you this, but Bettina and I won't be joining you and the others on the tour today."

"Marco, I'm so sorry to hear that. Is Bettina ill?"

"No," Marco hesitated, then responded in a downcast voice, "I've just received some devastating news about the business transaction we worked on the other day. I've been on the phone all morning with everyone I could think of who might be able to help me speed up the process, but so far, I haven't had any luck. I think it would just be better if I stayed on ship and continued to try to solve the issue."

"I'm so sorry to hear that," Kate said. "We will miss you and Bettina today, but I know you are making the right decision. You wouldn't enjoy the tour if you have problems on your mind. If there is anything I can do to help, please let me know."

"You are wonderful. Why don't we meet in the theater at six o'clock? I'll explain everything to you. And thanks for your offer of help. You belong to a vanishing group of wonderful human beings who are still willing to step in and help others. Enjoy the tour and don't worry about us. I'll talk to you later."

Kate said goodbye and hung up. She was worried about what Marco had told her but felt that with his business experience, he could work it all out. Grabbing her light raincoat and umbrella, she and Ellie headed out to meet the others for a light lunch.

Afterwards, everyone went downstairs to exit the ship. The heavy rainfall caused a delay in the start of the tour. Finally, they got a break and walked quickly down the gangplank to their waiting tour bus. The gray and dreary colors of the day gave the drive to the train a breathtaking view of the area. The coastline looked like a study in blacks, grays, and whites, with the turbulent dark waves breaking their white foam on the ebony-colored rocks along the beach. David sat next to Kate and remarked, "The whole sea has a different look on a cloudy, rainy day."

"I know. I was just thinking how beautiful everything looked, even though the skies are so dark. It just gives a different perspective to the beach."

Soon, they arrived at a railroad crossing, where they would climb aboard the train for the first leg of the tour. The narrow-gauge train was very old, with wooden seats and small windows. It looked like one from the early days of the Old West. She wondered if they might encounter actors playing train robbers along the tour like they do in the States. Since the windows were fogged over, everyone had to open them to see where they were going, which let the rain pour into the car.

Ellie and Adam started laughing and chanting in a childish singsong voice, "Rain, Rain go away; come again another day." Before long, their whole car was making jokes about the rain and how wet they were all getting. They all agreed that although the train ride was interesting and enjoyable, the warm and dry bus felt much better.

Next, they arrived at the dock area for the boat part of the tour. The rain was falling heavily again. The water had risen almost even with the dock. Everyone climbed aboard the boat and took their seats as they headed out on the river to see if they could spot any animal life or unusual birds. Before long, their tour director used a laser pointer to show the group where they could see a large sloth slowly moving through the upper branches of a tree.

Kate kept looking but couldn't find it until David put his arm around her shoulders and leaned over to point it out. The action caught her off guard at first, but once his arm was there, she found it a nice presence. Finally, she could see the lazy animal, munching on leaves from the tree, apparently oblivious to all the boats filled with tourists watching his every move. Kate smiled at David. Their eyes held for a moment before he moved his arm and sat up straight again, although a little more closely than before.

Amanda was laughing as she looked over at them. "That sloth reminds me of Adam as a kid when I had to wake him for school." Her playful teasing sparked laughter from their group and a few others.

Despite the rain, the boat ride was great. Everyone was having a good time.

Before they left the dock for the last leg of the tour, they had time to sample delicious and naturally sweet mangoes, papayas, melons, passion fruit, and bananas served on large platters on tables in the reception area. All the exquisite fruit had been grown in areas close by.

After boarding the bus, David sat very close to Kate to keep her from getting a chill, as their clothes were still damp from the rain. She welcomed his warmth and happily leaned against him as they headed out to view an agricultural area outside of Limon that was dotted with many large banana plantations. The heavily ladened trees lined both sides of the road. The stalks of bananas were individually wrapped in large blue plastic bags. The tour guide pointed out that workers had bagged all the fruit to protect it from damage by insects or animals. Some passengers on the bus asked how long it must have taken for the stalks to be wrapped and how many snakes the workers had found while they were working. One man remarked that he had a new appreciation for bananas after seeing the plantations.

The tour had really gone well. Kate felt warm and comfortable with David beside her as they headed back to the dock.

Just as the bus reached the parking area, the rain subsided, and the wet but happy passengers disembarked and headed back to the ship, ready for warm showers and a change of clothes. The dinner group made their way across the parking lot, laughing and holding hands as they jumped over the many rain puddles. They carefully walked up the gangplank and had their passenger ID cards scanned as they entered the ship.

Since it was getting close to 6:00 p.m. and time for Kate to meet Marco, she hurried to the stateroom to change into dry clothes. Ellie and Adam were going to meet in the arcade after changing while everyone else decided to take the time before dinner to get a little rest.

Kate quickly changed and called out to Ellie that she was leaving to meet Marco. She took the elevator down to the second deck to enter the darkened theater. As she went in, she could see a couple on the stage, practicing their dance routine. She stood in the lobby looking around until she saw Marco sitting near the exit. Kate rushed over to meet him.

"Marco, I hope I didn't keep you waiting."

"Ah, there you are. No, I just got here myself. How was the tour?"

"A little wet but otherwise very enjoyable. I've never seen so many bananas before." She laughed.

Marco looked tired and a little strained. "Let's walk over there, where we can talk and not be in the aisle."

Kate followed him to the side of the theater, where they were alone. "Marco, I've been worried about you. You sounded a little upset over the phone today. Is everything all right?"

"Not really," he replied. "I got some devastating news this morning from my company attorneys."

"Oh no, did the deal fall through?"

"No, everything is still in place. The problem is that instead of transferring the money directly to my business account, they have to wait until their in-house attorneys finalize the paperwork and process it through the bank in Colombia. Business laws here require that a company doing business with an American company must wait thirty days before any monetary transactions can be made. Bettina's treatments are scheduled to begin December 1 and payment for the treatment has to be received by the fifteenth of November. That is just ten days from now. I don't keep that much in my personal account, and with the pending investment in the company, my business account is frozen until the final paperwork is processed. I don't know what I am going to do. If they drop her from the patient program at the hospital, it could take months before she gets back up to the top of the list again. I have been beside myself all day and trying not to let her know the problems we have encountered. I've tried contacting friends and business associates but without any luck so far. Kate, I'm scared. I don't know what to do." He turned away and wiped tears from his eyes.

She gently laid her hand on his shoulder. "Don't worry. Let me see what I can do. There must be some way to work with the hospital."

Marco shook his head. "No, I've already tried to reason with them and told them I could send a post-dated check for the twenty-five thousand dollars they need, but they said they do not accept post-dated checks. The frustrating thing is that it is only for a couple of weeks. After that, the two million dollars from the investment will be transferred, and the amount the hospital needs would be easily covered."

"Marco, I'll try to help you. The amount you need is twenty-five thousand dollars?"

"Yes," he replied. "But Kate, I can't accept any help from you. We have just met, and even though I feel closer to you than I have with any other woman, I won't involve you in this problem. You have your life, and I don't want to cause you any distress or upset. You are too kind and caring, and I would never take advantage of you."

"Marco, let me worry about whether you are taking advantage of me or not. The primary concern is Bettina's health. Let me think a little. I might be able to work something out. Just give me a day to get in touch with my bank."

Marco turned and put his hands on her shoulders. "Kate, I don't know what to say. You are definitely an angel. I have never met anyone like you. Just talking to you makes me feel better. I'll never know how to thank you enough. I'll talk to you tomorrow. Bettina and I are just going to stay in our room. With all this going on, I really don't have much of an appetite."

They stood together, eyes locked in their seductive dance. Then he leaned down and pulled her to him, kissing her soundly. After the kiss, he continued to hold her close for a long moment. He then took a step back and looked at her with an expression she couldn't define. It was almost a look of regret and sadness.

"I'm sorry. I really shouldn't have done that." He turned and hurriedly left the theater.

Kate stood there not fully understanding what had just happened. Perhaps Marco was just upset over Bettina, and there wasn't some hidden meaning in his eyes.

Since it seemed they weren't going to have dance practice, Kate stood there a moment contemplating her next move. Still a little confused over what had transpired with Marco, she returned to the stateroom and began organizing her notes for the final chapter that she hoped to write tomorrow.

After diligently working, she looked at her watch and realized it was almost time for dinner. Ellie and Adam were in the game room and would meet the group in the dining room. Tonight, the chef had a surprise menu prepared for the guests.

As Kate entered the dining room, she saw everyone was already there. She took her usual seat next to David as they all discussed their tours for the next day. The ship would be in port in Cancun, but Kate had been there several times before and wanted to use the quiet port time to concentrate on writing. David, Oscar, and Amanda had booked a city tour and were planning to make a couple of stops at Señor Frog's and Jimmy Buffett's restaurants. David mentioned that these stops were purely in the interest of science to determine which place had the best margaritas. Kate had told them that they all would probably be standing on the bus doing the 'Macarena' before they got back to the ship. David finally turned to Kate and asked, "Have you heard from Marco and Bettina?"

"They won't be joining us tonight." Kate shook her head.

Amanda looked concerned. "I hope they aren't ill again."

"No," Kate responded. "Marco received some bad news about his business dealings in Cartagena, and they didn't feel very social tonight."

"That's a shame," Amanda replied. "People shouldn't have to worry about business when they're on vacation, and they are going to miss the surprise dinner."

"It's a little more serious than just a business deal. Without going into all the details, Bettina is ill, and they were hoping that the investor in Colombia would help with the enormous expenses of her treatment. Now, it looks like the timing is not going to work out. I told him that if he liked, I would try to help him come up with a solution."

David quickly chimed in, "Not with money, I hope."

Ellie laughed. "Ha! That would be very difficult. My grandmother is locked up tighter than Fort Knox when it comes to giving people money. When I was little, I had to have some kind of collateral to borrow a dollar for the popsicle truck."

Kate rolled her eyes. "Elle, that's not true. I just know that women my age are susceptible to scams, and I want to make sure that everything is on the up and up before I throw any monetary help at people. I would be the first person to help someone that was truly in need, but it would have to be done correctly and with my attorney's approval. No, I have some friends in the hospital system in Houston that might be able to offer a solution."

"That's kind of you to get involved when you are on vacation too. I hope everything works out for them," Oscar said.

The waiters brought the appetizers to the table, proudly saying, "We have something special tonight. Where are the other two guests?"

David explained that Marco and Bettina wouldn't be joining them tonight, but they were sorry they would miss out on this dinner. All eyes turned to the trays that held the first course of the menu.

"It's fried oysters again!" Kate happily exclaimed. Marco was surely missing out on another good meal. "Those were so good the last time we had them. The chef really knows how to keep us happy."

"I'm sorry that Marco and Bettina aren't here to join us," Ellie said. "I remember he said that he loved oysters the first night they were served and was sorry he wasn't feeling well enough to eat."

Kate dipped her golden mollusks into the cocktail sauce. "I have an idea. Since they aren't here, I'll have the waiter fix a tray that I could take to their room as a surprise."

"I can carry the tray for you," Adam added.

"Great, let's see what else is on our surprise menu tonight. We might add another dish to our tray. Adam, when we get to their room, you knock and tell them that you're maintenance and need to check for a leak in their room. Then we can carry the tray in and—"

Ellie interjected, "Please tell me you aren't going to yell, 'Surprise.'"

"No, we'll be a little more low-key than that. It will just be a gesture to show that we are thinking of them and want them to be able to enjoy the best oysters in the world one last time on this cruise. Maybe the next course will be onion soup. Remember how great that was?" Happy with the idea, Kate finished the appetizer and waited for the next course, which did turn out to be the ship's famous onion soup, complete with lots of melted Swiss cheese on top and toasted croutons.

"Kate, you must be a mind reader. I think I'll let you pick out my lottery numbers." David winked at her.

Everyone laughed. Kate was glad Marco's two favorite dishes were on the menu tonight. *This must be a sign that me taking a tray to him is a good idea.*

The main course turned out to be a surf and turf combo, with succulent lobster and drawn butter served with a petite filet topped with a rich blue cheese sauce. Steamed broccoli accompanied the plate, and there were plenty of wonderful fresh-baked rolls to complete the course. Crème brûlée was served for dessert. After dinner, they all enjoyed a cup of herbal tea or coffee, satisfied with the meal.

Time to put their plan into motion. Kate called the waiter over and asked if she could have a tray to take as a surprise for Marco and Bettina. The waiter told her he would have someone take the tray to the room if she liked.

"No, we are going to do it as a surprise to let them know how much we missed their company tonight. Could you give them two orders of appetizers and two large bowls of that delicious onion soup?" Kate asked.

"Of course," the waiter said. "We will add two desserts as well."

"Thank you so much. I know that will cheer them up."

As the waiter left, the group turned back to their discussion of tomorrow's adventures while they waited for the tray to arrive.

Chapter Sixteen

Marco

The cabin occupied by Marco and Bettina was quiet and lit by only a small desk lamp. Bettina was comfortably lying in bed while Marco stood at the small bedside table, lost in thought.

"Sam, come to bed. Momma's getting anxious."

"Bettina," Marco retorted sharply, "I've told you to call me Marco while we're on the ship. You're going to slip at some point and mess up everything."

"Come on, baby, don't be angry." Her bottom lip stuck out a little and her eyes beseeched him. It wasn't her fault he was troubled. She ran a hand along the bedspread, gaze roaming up and down his body as if he were a plaything. "Did you take your little blue pill yet?"

Irritated by her question, he answered sharply. "Yes, I should think you would have noticed."

"Well, I might if you would just get in bed. You seem a little distracted tonight. How did the meeting with Kate go? Do you think she bought it?"

"It went well. I'm just not happy with this one. Kate is really a nice woman. I hate to take advantage of her."

"What?" Bettina frowned as she sat up a little. "Don't tell me you're getting a conscience this late in the game. How much did you ask for?"

"I said we only needed twenty-five thousand dollars to start the treatment and that I would give a post-dated check to the person who wanted to help. I didn't come right out and ask; that would have put her on guard. We have to make her think that helping us is her idea, or the scam won't work. Intelligent dames are difficult to trick."

Bettina leaned back on the pillow. "Wow! Twenty-five thousand bucks. We've never made that much before."

"We've never been lucky enough to have a mark like this one before. That's on you. If you hadn't read her novels and followed her on Facebook, we'd never have known that she was going to be on this ship."

"Yeah, but you were the one who convinced our tour agent that we wanted to surprise our cousin Kate and be seated with her at dinner. I tell you, Sa-...*Marco*, when you put that hairpiece on, you can charm the world." Bettina laughed as she looked over at him standing beside the bed, wearing only a pair of thin flannel pajama bottoms. "Baby, it looks like the pharmaceuticals are working. Come to bed, and let's celebrate."

Marco stepped out of the pajamas and was crawling into bed when he heard a knock on the door and someone shout, "Maintenance! We need to check your room for a water leak. It will only take a second."

"Damn! They couldn't have picked a worse time." He jumped out of bed, pulled on the pajama bottoms, and went to the door. As he opened the door and turned to head back to the bed, he heard Kate's voice. "Surprise! Adam and I brought you a gift you are going to love."

Kate

Kate crossed the room with Adam's help to place the tray on the desk. Once the tray was in place, she stood up straight and smiled at Marco.

A very bald Marco.

The smile quickly dropped as she glanced around the room.

"Marco," she demanded. "What's going on here? Where is your hair?" She glanced at the bedside table, where the bottle of blue pills was conspicuously displayed. Looking at Marco in his thin flannel pajama pants, she could see the effects of the pills. Marco saw her glance at his body and quickly grabbed a pillow to place in front of the evidence. She turned her glare to Bettina, who pulled up the bedcovers.

"I don't understand." Kate's voice was growing louder. Anger seethed within her as her mind processed everything she was seeing. "Please tell me you're not sleeping with your sister!"

Standing beside her, Adam whispered quietly, "I'm just going over to my cabin now. I'll leave the door open in case you need anything." Then he slipped quickly out of the room to the corridor, where his parents and Ellie were waiting. Kate continued staring at Marco, immobilized and struggling to sort out what was happening in front of her.

"This is sick. For the first time in my life, I'm completely at a loss for words." Her loud voice and disgusted look made Marco cringe.

"Kate, it's not what you think," Marco said. She could tell he was scrambling to gain control of the situation. "Let me explain."

Bettina sat up in bed and quickly pulled the sheet over her unclothed body. "Sam, give it up. She's on to us."

"Sam?" Kate asked sharply. "Who the hell is Sam? What is going on here? Who are you people?"

A million upsetting thoughts raced through her mind and filled her with anger and outrage. She had been played, just as she'd always been so careful to avoid, and that knowledge brought a sense of indignation and disappointment that filled her whole body.

"I'm waiting for an explanation." She could barely keep her voice civil.

Sam, or Marco, or whatever his name was tried to speak, but Bettina looked at him with sad eyes. "It's over, Sam." She then turned to Kate and with a defeated voice said, "We are Sam and Betty. He's not my brother. He's my husband and has been for thirty-five years. We were just having a little fun with you and didn't mean any harm."

Still standing by the desk where she and Adam had placed the tray, Kate struggled to keep her fury in check. Hands on hips and fire sparking out of her eyes, she snapped, "Fun! You call it fun when you misrepresent yourselves? You took advantage of everyone at our table. You took advantage of my trust and friendship. Everything you said and did was a lie. Why? Was this all a scam just to get money from me? Is there any part of your story that is true? Marco, are you even Italian?"

Betty laughed sarcastically. "Well, if being a waiter at Antonini's Italian Garden qualifies him to be Italian, then I guess he is."

"Shut up, Betty. You're only making it worse." Sam stood with a white-knuckled grip on the pillow he held.

"Oh, it can't be worse, trust me. Is this something the two of you do all the time? Do you go on cruises just to find lonely, old women you can shakedown with your schemes? How did you pick me? Was I just a lucky find, or did you plan beforehand to meet me on this trip?" The rising anger threatened to choke Kate with its intensity. She'd been such a fool.

Sam had that strange look on his face that he had when they met earlier that evening. He kept his eyes downcast and seemed almost remorseful over his actions. She should have trusted her instincts.

"Betty has read all of your books and follows you on social media. We knew from your Facebook page you would be taking a cruise. With just a few hints, I was able to figure out which ship you would be on," he replied softly. "I managed to get us seated with you for dinner by telling the dining room manager that I was your cousin and wanted to surprise you."

Kate shook her head incredulously. "So, all of the time we spent together was just part of the con? The story about your sister's cancer and needing twenty-five thousand dollars for treatment was the bait I was supposed to grab. What I don't understand is, did you really think that I am so stupid I would have written a large check and given it to someone I had just met? If the story had been true, I am in a position to help, but it wouldn't have been with money." She took a deep breath and was struck by a painful thought. A wave of sadness eroded the anger as she remembered all the times they had spent together. "And what about the dancing, the walks on the deck, the talks we shared—was all of it nothing but a sham?"

"Not all of it was a sham." His face fell, and his voice lost the beauty it once held. "I enjoyed the dancing. Kate, you really are a wonderful dancer. I truly hoped we would win the ship's contest. You deserve that."

She looked directly at him, his words tapping back into her anger. "But there's something else you did that went a little too far. It went deeper and was more personal. Tonight, you kissed me. What about the kiss? Was that part of the script?"

Hearing that, Betty sat up even straighter and glared at him. "What kiss? You kissed her?"

Sam stood there, looking a little uneasy. He shifted back and forth on his feet while still holding the pillow in place. "Betty, it was just a little peck. It didn't mean anything."

Kate shot back, "Oh no, it wasn't just a little peck! It was a total lip-lock, full-body-contact kiss. A woman knows when she is really being kissed. I could feel it."

"What do you mean you felt it?" Betty glanced at Kate, then not waiting for a response, released her rage on Sam. "What is she talking about, Sam? What did she feel?"

"Betty, she didn't feel anything. It wasn't a big deal." Sam began to look a little more nervous as he looked between the two women.

"No big deal?" Kate yelled. "I beg to differ. When anyone kisses me, it is always a big deal. I'm not some desperate, lonely, old woman just waiting to be rescued by the first man who shows me any attention. I have a life, and I have all the attention I want. But your kiss was filled with passion and desire. You might not want to admit that in front of your wife, but it's true. You also had a little remorse in your eyes when you ran from the theater."

Sam stood between the two women, looking like he wanted to bolt at any minute and make a run for the door. Kate stared at him with fire in her eyes. The man squirmed beneath her gaze. She turned and saw the wig stand on the desk with Marco's hairpiece pinned to it, along with a Panama hat with a bright pink floral band and pink feather.

She leaned over and touched the hat. "So, you *were* the 'Macarena' man we saw." Before she thought about it, she heard words coming from her mouth she never would have said. "Ye not be flying a true flag, Marco. Ye be a scalawag and a trickster." She quietly muttered under her breath, "Edward, I can handle this. Please don't get involved."

Sam looked quizzically at her. "Why are you talking like a pirate, Kate?"

"I don't know. It just feels right when I'm dealing with the likes of you two. You really are flying a false flag, Marco, or Sam, or whoever the devil you are." She reached over and picked up the hairpiece.

Sam started to drop the pillow and move toward her but froze, choosing to hold the pillow in place considering his current condition. "Kate, don't touch the hair. It's a three-hundred-dollar custom-made toupee. Please be careful."

"Really?" She turned the hairpiece over in her hands. Looking at his face, she could tell that he was genuinely concerned about the toupee. A wicked thought crossed her mind. "Oh look, it has a little dirt on it." Holding the hair over the top of the onion soup and looking directly at Sam, Kate said, "We really need to take care of that."

Throwing caution to the wind, Sam dropped the pillow and rushed towards her. But before he could reach her, she had removed the top from one of the bowls of onion soup and plunged the hairpiece into the still-steaming liquid. She pushed it down past the croutons, through the melted cheese, and straight into the savory broth and caramelized onions. Slowly, she pulled the soaking toupee out of the bowl and held it so the melted cheese, croutons, and broth could drip on the tray.

"This isn't a hairpiece. It's the false flag that you fly." As she spoke, Kate drew back and, taking careful aim, threw the dripping mess directly at Sam's midsection. Her aim was true. "Run that up the flagpole you're sporting! I don't ever want to see the two of you again. I will inform the cruise manager of what happened. I hope you are confined to your room until we are back in Galveston again. But whatever happens, stay out of my sight!"

With as much aplomb as she could muster given the circumstances, Kate turned on her heel and marched out of the room, slamming the door hard enough that the sound reverberated through the corridor. She barely made it through the door before the deluge of tears that had been building up started flowing down her cheeks. All she wanted to do was get outside on deck and collapse on one of the couches. As she fled down the hall, past the open door to Oscar and Amanda's stateroom, she heard Ellie's voice calling her. But she wasn't in the mood for comfort or company, so she kept walking towards the exit doors. She heard Amanda tell Ellie that her grandma needed to be alone now.

Kate made it through the exit doors and headed to a couch in the seating area. Fortunately, the area was empty. She crumpled on a couch farthest from the doors and let the tears continue to fall. How could she have been so stupid?

I'm just a foolish old woman. There'll never be a man in my life at this point. I'll never have the connection I've dreamed of for so long. I just don't understand why. What is wrong with me?

Her thoughts and feelings tumbled within her as the cushion soaked up her tears. With her emotions running rampant in her head and deep sobs controlling her body, Kate concluded that the only thing left to do was accept her loneliness and inability to find someone to love her. The days of sweeping romance and grand gestures were long past her. The only thing left for her was a lingering emptiness in her life, a void that would never be filled by any other man.

She leaned against the couch, letting herself be completely immersed in the sadness she felt.

Chapter Seventeen

"Kate, is that you?" David asked, concern in his voice.

Kate sniffled a couple of times. "David, I'm really not good company now. I think I just need to be alone for a little while."

"I understand," David replied. "I want to make sure you're okay. You don't need to talk. Let me sit beside you and just be here for you. No talking, no explanations, nothing at all. Just support if you need it."

She could feel his body as he sat next to her, even though she refused to open her eyes. Despite wanting to be alone, having him there brought her a small measure of comfort. They sat for a few silent minutes.

"I really don't want to talk about it, but I am so upset I just have to say something, or I'll burst. But I'm afraid of what you will think of me." Avoiding eye contact, but not his offered comfort, she leaned her head against his shoulder.

"I'll think of you just the way I think of you now. You can trust me to listen to whatever you need to say." He wrapped an arm around her shoulders. She could tell by his voice that he was truly concerned but did not want to intrude on her feelings.

"I know, David. You are so accepting and non-judgmental, and I'm such a pathetic old fool. Marco is a fraud and a con man. He was trying to scam me into giving him money. When we took the tray to their stateroom, we caught him and Bettina in a very compromising position. When I asked for an explanation, she said Marco was her husband. His name was really Sam, and her name was Betty." She began to sob again. "He just wanted money from me. I guess he thought I was lonely enough that if he tossed me a few crumbs of attention, I would fall willingly into his scheme. Everything he did—the attention he showed me, the dancing, the deep conversations, everything—was just to gain my trust, and I fell for it like the desperate woman I guess I am." As she spoke, her sobs increased, and she turned away. "I really can't talk about it."

Without saying anything, David offered her a handkerchief, which she took without comment. Her tears flowed freely, the sobs preventing any conversation.

After a few long minutes, she blew her nose and wiped her eyes. "And…there's more. He isn't Italian. He's actually bald, and oh yes, he *was* the 'Macarena' man on the party bus. I saw the Panama hat with the pink feather in his room. He and Betty are professional scammers, who prey on older, lonely women. I can't believe I trusted him!" She wiped the fresh tears from her eyes and dabbed her nose again. The handkerchief was fairly soaked from her crying, but she didn't care. Encouraged by David's quiet listening, she told him the thing that hurt the most. "And with everything else, he kissed me!"

"He kissed you?" She could hear the irritation in his voice as he tensed beneath her. "You mean like a peck on the cheek?"

"No," Kate sobbed, "a full man-woman kiss. He tried to tell Betty it wasn't anything, but I know better. He planted one on me, looked at me strangely, then ran out of the theater. That just wasn't right. He shouldn't have taken advantage of my personal feelings while he was trying to scam me. I was so mad when I thought about the kiss, I took his expensive toupee and dunked it into the French Onion soup!" A small smile tugged at her lips at the memory. "Edward warned me Marco wasn't an honorable man, but I didn't believe him. I should have listened. He was right."

"Seriously, you dipped his toupee in the soup?" David turned towards her, so she was forced to look at him. A spark of humor lit his eyes.

"Well, not exactly dipped, it was more like submerging the whole thing into the bowl until it was completely soaked."

"Oh boy, it's going to take some work to get all the melted cheese and onions out, and the smell will probably linger for a while." He tried to keep his composure out of respect for Kate, but he couldn't hold it anymore. David laughed so hard he could barely speak. She smiled but couldn't quite join in his merriment. After a few moments, he stopped and turned serious. "Wait! Did you say Edward warned you about Marco? You mean your pirate Edward?"

Kate sank into the couch and sighed when she realized what she had said. "Oh no, I didn't mean to say that. Now you're going to think I'm not only lamentable but also crazy."

He took her hand. "Kate, I could never think you are crazy; highly imaginative and creative maybe, but not crazy. However, I am curious about Edward. Do the two of you speak often? Does his voice just appear, or do you have to contact him?"

She hesitated. She had only told Ellie about her nocturnal visits from an imaginary pirate, and she wasn't sure if David would understand. On the other hand, he did seem trustworthy and had shown he had her best interests at heart. Maybe it wouldn't hurt to tell him.

"All right, I guess I owe you an explanation. Let me start from the beginning." Kate dove into the story, telling David all about her struggles with finding pirate inspiration. She told him about the storm, and the night Edward first appeared to her. "After that night, he began to visit me while I was sleeping every so often until the book was finished. I thought he had gone for good, but a few months after the book had become a bestseller, he appeared again and said it was time for us to get started on our second book. It's crazy. I know he's only a product of my dreams and my subconscious, but he's starting to feel like a friend."

Having made her confession, she leaned forward and put her face in her hands.

"You know, I can't say I've ever been close friends with a fiction writer, but I can only imagine many of them have similar stories. How else can someone come up with such vivid characters and lives on their own?" David said.

Kate looked up at him, and in his face, she saw nothing but acceptance. "Thank you, David."

The events of the evening were beginning to weigh heavily on her. She was feeling a little tired from everything that had transpired. As she reviewed the day in her mind, she sat up and looked at David with alarm.

"Oh no! The dance contest. Without that scoundrel, I won't be in the contest. I was really looking forward to performing our dances, and now everything's ruined!" She slumped back onto the cushions, what remaining energy she had left lay crushed on her shattered dreams.

David took her hand and softly replied, "If you like, I can be your partner for the contest."

Kate looked at him through teary eyes. "You dance?"

"Well, my wife thought I spent way too much time with my head either in a book or in the night sky, so she signed us up for ballroom dance classes. We really liked it and even won a few contests around the state. I used to dance a mean Charleston, and our tango was banned in seven counties." He laughed, but she could tell he was only half-joking.

"You would really be my partner, even after finding out I am an emotional hot mess?" Hope lifted her spirits. Not only had David not run away during her emotional crisis, but he'd offered to repair some of the damage that scoundrel had done.

"Kate, I don't think you really qualify as an emotional hot mess; more like a kind and trusting woman with a wonderful imagination."

His words warmed her heart. "This is wonderful. You and the unspeakable person are about the same size, so his costumes will probably fit you. We have all of tomorrow and a little time the next day before the contest to practice. I will tell Casey what is going on. I'm sure she would be fine with the substitution." Kate turned and grasped David's hands in enthusiasm. "This is unbelievable. A minute ago, I thought my life was destined to be mired in a drab, boring existence, but you just put all the fun back into it!"

"I'm happy I was able to help you tonight, Kate. Don't feel any guilt in befriending Marco. He is a practiced con man.

Anyone would have taken him at his word and not been suspicious. You have a beautiful, loving heart, and he took advantage of your natural warmth and empathy towards other people. At least you were smart enough to not even consider giving him money. That shows you are a very intelligent and shrewd woman. Marco is a professional. He had all of us fooled. Don't let that experience with him change the way you respond to people. Stay the same sweet, loving person you are now."

She smiled and ducked her head. His compliments felt different than Marco's, maybe because his were sincere. "Thank you. I do feel foolish, but I guess you are right. A person can't go through life always being suspicious of others. It just wouldn't make for a very happy existence. I appreciate your support tonight. I hope I never see Marco again in my life!"

"I imagine Marco will spend the rest of the cruise picking sautéed onions and cheese out of his hairpiece," David joked. "Seriously, though, I'm glad I could help, but I'm really confused. When I first sat down, you said you didn't want to talk, but then you started talking and talking, and that's got me wondering. If tonight was an example of what you're like when you don't want to talk, what on earth are you like when you do?" he asked in mock fear, eyebrows raised.

Kate playfully slapped his arm. "Professor Mitchell, are you saying that I talk too much?" Laughing, she leaned against his shoulder for a few moments before he spoke.

"Time to get you back to your cabin, young lady." He stood and held out his hand. "You've had quite the night. You better get some rest if you want to keep up with me tomorrow on the dance floor."

"And who put you in charge?" She asked before taking his offered hand to stand beside him.

David put his arm around her as they headed back inside but dropped it to open the door for her. The elevator came quickly, and he walked her all the way to her stateroom. When they reached her door, she turned to him and took his hand.

"David, you have been my salvation tonight. You listened without admonishing me for being so stupid. You didn't outwardly show that you think I am crazy when I told you about Edward, and then, you astonished me by volunteering to be my dance partner. You are a true jewel. Thank you for everything." Kate leaned forward and kissed him gently on the lips before saying, "Good night."

David smiled down at her. Taking both of her hands in his, he kissed each one while gazing directly into her eyes. "Good night, Kate. I'll see you tomorrow afternoon." Then, he headed down the corridor to his stateroom.

Kate watched him walk away. She was overcome by a newfound happiness she had not had in many years. She opened the door and walked into the stateroom.

"Grandma! I've been so worried about you. Are you okay?" Ellie's frantic voice matched the tears streaming down her cheeks as she stood to greet Kate before she'd made it past the threshold.

Kate held her granddaughter in a tight embrace. "Elle, I'm just fine. In fact, I think I'm better than I have been in ages.

This has been a whirlwind of a night. You can never guess what happened."

Ellie stood back to scrutinize her grandmother's face as if she couldn't believe what Kate had said. "We all heard what happened with Marco. I'm so sorry he turned out to be a con artist."

"Oh, Marco doesn't even exist for me anymore." Kate dismissed the scoundrel with a wave of her hand. "I discovered someone much better."

"Wait. You've already found someone new? In only a couple of hours?" Ellie's incredulous look made Kate laugh.

"Well, it really isn't someone new. While I was having my pity party for one on the deck, David came and sat with me. We talked about everything involved with Marco's deception. David was wonderful about the whole thing and never once made me feel like I had been stupid for not seeing through Marco. He was so concerned and patient with me. He listened. When I realized that discovering who Marco really was would cause me to miss the dance competition, I was even more devastated. Surprisingly, David and his wife had been active ballroom dancers. He volunteered to be my partner in the dance contest. And if that wasn't enough to prove what an understanding and kind person David is, I accidentally mentioned something about Edward's visits, and he didn't think I was crazy at all. It turned out to be a wonderful evening."

"Wow. David sounds even more wonderful than I ever thought," Ellie said.

Kate smiled and nodded, but she was too tired to talk about it anymore. "Now, young lady, you've got an early tour in the morning, and I've got writing to do, so let's head to bed and get a good night's sleep. After the evening we've had, I think we both need the rest."

"Wait, you said David and his wife danced. Is David married?" Ellie's face scrunched up in confusion. Kate had seen that look many times before. It was funny what didn't change as one grew.

"No, he was. His wife passed away over three years ago."

"Grandma, what I still don't understand is, after the incident with Marco, I thought you would be devastated and upset. Instead, you seem almost elated with the whole evening. I guess it must have something to do with age. If that happened to me, I would be in bed for a week crying my eyes out."

"No, it's not age. It's just experience from years of living. You learn to discard the bad feelings and appreciate the good ones—you know, the feelings I have when I'm with you." Kate gave Ellie a hug then walked to her room. She was tired.

Before entering her room, Ellie called to her, "Grandma, I love you more than you could ever know. I'm so glad you are happy."

The next morning, Kate looked out the window by her bed and saw that the weather had cleared up. It was going to be a beautiful day. She dressed and went out on the balcony to start writing. The final chapter was always exciting. This one was even more so since Edward would be taking Millie with him and sailing off to his adventurous life at sea.

Kate was a little apprehensive as to how her readers would accept Edward having an ongoing romance but rationalized that they could each imagine that they were with him in Millie's place. Sales would tell. If this went well, then by the fourth book, everyone would be interested to see if he stayed with Millie or returned to his carefree bachelor ways. Thinking it over, she realized that maybe she was the one who was a little apprehensive about Edward's romance with Millie.

Chapter Eighteen

THE FIERY PASSION OF A
THOUSAND BURNING SUNS

Edward

The sailors tied up the sleek Spanish galleon to the mooring with ease. They had reached Southampton. Receiving Edward's dispatch, the grand duke had sailed for England to wait the arrival of his niece. Having just arrived themselves during the early morning hours, Edward and Millie walked out on the deck of the Falcon *and met Henry and Lady Teresa, who had been watching the ship dock. Lady Teresa looked anxiously at the people leaving the boat, searching for an emissary from her uncle who would accompany her on the voyage to Seville. Henry stood protectively at her side, looking a little distracted. He must feel the same sense of dread Edward felt about parting with Millie, if she changed her mind.*

Edward went to stand beside them, the lovely Millie standing close by. Her presence beside him felt right.

"Uncle, Uncle! I'm over here." Lady Teresa waved to an elderly aristocrat on the pier.

Edward was surprised to see that Alphonso Lopez, the grand duke himself, had come to take his niece home. As both parties met on the pier, the grand duke grabbed Lady Teresa and pulled her into a giant hug. "Teresa, mi Cariña, ¿estás bien?"

Lady Teresa smiled at her uncle. "Sí, Tio. Eran muy amables."

The grand duke faced Edward and shook his hand. "Edward, I'm so thankful you were able to get to the ship in time. I was told another ship had been following the Santa Magdalena. I shudder to think what might have happened if you hadn't interceded."

"Señor Lopez, I be happy to help. Ye have a fine niece, and I know ye have a strong fondness for the young lady. Me crew and me be honored to return her to ye unharmed." Edward leaned over and whispered, "She be unharmed, but it appears she might have found a suitor on the trip."

Lady Teresa and Henry stood beside the coach, looking sad, eyes locked on one another.

An excited voice shouted, "Edward, is that you?"

Edward looked over his shoulder and saw Norman rushing towards him. Norman had not been at the office during the time they had waited for the galleon. This was the first that Edward had seen his brother.

"Aye, Norman," Edward responded. "It be me."

The two brothers greeted each other with handshakes and pats on the back.

"Let me look at my young brother." Norman stood back and gazed up, as he stood a head shorter than Edward. "How long has it been, Edward?"

"Evidently, it be long enough for ye to learn proper English speak," Edward teased.

"And I see you still use the old language. But you still are a good bràthair. I guess the old Scottish speak bodes well with the ladies," Norman bantered. "Alphonso, it's good to see you again. Come everyone, let's go to my office and share a wee dram of some good Scotch whisky while we catch up."

The group walked the short distance to the shipping company's office and sat in comfortable, upholstered, mahogany Chippendale chairs around a large matching mahogany table. Norman retrieved a tray with a bottle of Scotch and six glasses that had been placed on an ornately carved chest near the table. He poured the amber-colored liquid into the glasses, careful to only give the ladies half as much as the men. As the last glass was filled, Edward raised his tumbler and offered the traditional Scottish toast, Slàinte mhath. Glasses clinked together before everyone took a taste of the full-flavored refreshment.

"How are things in the colonies now?" Norman asked.

Before Edward could answer, the grand duke pointed out that business discussions might bore the ladies. Lady Teresa and Millie agreed to visit the fashionable dress shops in the area. Norman went to the door and called to one of his assistants to accompany the ladies on their shopping journey.

"Whatever you purchase, put on my account," Norman told the ladies.

Señor Lopez laughed. "You might be sorry you made that offer. Young women have been known to find many things that they can't live without."

Lady Teresa playfully made a face at her uncle as she and Millie left the office. Norman returned to the table with a box of Cuban cigars. Seeing the box, Alphonso looked surprised. "You must have paid a pretty penny for these. King Philip keeps a tight control on his tobacco products."

Norman passed the cigars around the table. "Actually, Philip sent these to me as a gift for helping move some of the tobacco and cigars from Cuba to Seville after one of his ships was unable to leave the Cuban port due to needed repairs. His majesty was very generous. I still have several boxes stored in a special humidor at my home."

The Cohiba cigar was a sweet and mild cigar with hints of caramel, grass, and a light wheat. Edward leaned back in his chair, crossed his legs, and propped his feet on the table. Looking up at the ceiling, he drew on the cigar and exhaled a perfect smoke ring that floated over his head. Satisfied with his accomplishment, he said, "Ye asked about conditions in the colonies. It not be good now. The pirates have ports in Jamaica, Haiti, and Nassau, and they be freely roaming the seas and pillaging the smaller villages on the islands. Many smaller islands be overrun with ragtags and bobtails. Those lowlifes take whatever they want. They show no quarter to the people who live there."

The anger he felt became more apparent as he continued. "I be hearing that many of Britain's privateers, who be relieved of military duty, turned to pirating as a way of making a living. The pirate captains have no need to train these seamen, who be seeking their fortunes rather than serving their country. Now, with the slave ships bringing Africans to work the fields in the colonies, merchant ships be taking more and more goods and valuables back to Spain and England. The pirates have a good number of targets for their taking."

"That does sound bad," Norman said. "I have heard that the British Royal Navy is sending a squadron to Port Royal to help protect the trade routes. This will probably make it more difficult for the privateers to get letters of marque. If that is the case, the ships should be safer in their voyages, and you, dear Edward, could come home and take your rightful place in our company."

"Aye, I be hearing the same thing," Edward said in a voice more frustrated than angry. He took a long inhale of the cigar and allowed the deep breath to relax him. "Safe trade routes will help, but they not be the final answer for the colonies. They still be robbed of all their silver, gold, and jewels. What the governments be doing will only help their own countries and not the indigenous people of the islands. The colonies be needing leadership that focuses on the needs of the people who be living there. The slaves in Colombia be revolting against the living conditions and be fleeing to the mountains to form palenques, where they can live like in Africa."

"I know Philip is instigating many reforms in the colonies by trying to centralize the power of the monarchy with his Nueva Planta decrees," Señor Lopez said. "There are rumors Philip could give the throne to his eldest son, Louis, due to the long war over the Spanish succession to the crown. This has caused considerable unrest in the country."

"It be true that Philip be having more control of the colonies and lowering the power of the Council of the Indies, and he be also abolishing the House of Trade. With the new Viceroyalty of New Granada established, I be hearing they may be wanting to move the capital. With all that unrest, other countries be sending more trade ships to the area, and the colonies be depleted of anything of value. Sugar is growing in demand in Europe, and all through the islands, plantations be built. They be bringing in more slaves. The situation not be good at this time. I feel there may be a revolution in the making." Edward paused for a moment to think about the plan forming in his mind. "Norman, I be thinking that Henry might like to see the offices here and visit the auditorium, where ye be training the navigators for our ships."

Norman rose from his chair. "We just received the new government publications for navigation that will replace the British English Pilot. You might want to look them over."

Henry grinned. "I had heard there would be new publications but did not know they were in print already. I would greatly appreciate seeing them."

Both men left the office, chatting excitedly as they headed down the hall.

"Señor Lopez, we cannae solve the problems the government be having. However, I be wanting to enlighten ye to a new subject that needs to be discussed." Edward finished his Scotch and leaned forward in his chair.

"Of course. What would that be?"

Edward cleared his throat. "Well, it seems that Lady Teresa and my navigator, Henry Armitage, have developed a fondness for each other. I be thinking that the lady might like to have Henry stay in Seville, so they can continue their friendship. I be vouching for Henry's integrity and good moral character."

Alphonso smiled. "I did notice a lot of tender glances between the two. Lady Teresa is reaching the age of marriage but has not found a suitor to her liking until now. With your recommendation, perhaps Henry could become a member of the government navigation training in Seville. He could assist with classroom instruction. That would give the two of them time to see if they truly are in love and give Spain an excellent instructor to help our new naval recruits sail as safely as possible."

Edward smiled. "That be wonderful. Will ye be proposing this when we be all together?"

"I think that is the perfect time for the offer. I'm glad we have had this opportunity to talk, Edward. I look forward to the day when you can freely sail into the port of Seville for a visit. I know Philip does not harbor any resentment against you. The day will come when piracy will be a thing of the past. Hopefully, reforms will be instituted to provide for the native peoples of all the colonies."

Just as the discussion ended, the ladies came down the hall, laughing.

"We had a wonderful time." Lady Teresa burst happily into the room. "We found beautiful bolts of silks and velvets to have made into dresses when we return to Seville."

"This will protect my skin from the sun." Millie proudly displayed a beautiful straw brim hat with long chiffon ties on each side.

Norman's men followed with a towering set of packages. As the ladies were organizing their packages, Norman and Henry entered the room. Lady Teresa smiled when she looked at Henry, but it didn't reach her eyes.

Alphonso stood up and approached Henry. "My boy, Edward has been telling me wonderful things about you and your abilities as a navigator. I was wondering if perhaps you might be interested in accompanying Lady Teresa and myself back to Seville, where you would be commissioned as a member of King Philip's Royal Naval Training School to help train future seamen in the art of navigation."

Henry looked surprised and confused. He had not openly thought of leaving the Falcon, or Edward. His puzzled gaze landed on his captain to try to gauge his reaction to the grand duke's proposal. The decision was not one to be made without thinking everything through, and Edward respected his friend's careful consideration.

Seeing Henry's hesitancy, Edward walked over and placed his arm around the man's shoulders. "Henry, I be the one to suggest this possibility. I know this be a consternation to ye, but I told Alphonso that I be thinking ye be the best navigational instructor he could find. Ye be doing a service for all sailors, especially those who be new to the sea."

"But who would be the navigator on the Falcon? I worry about what would become of you and the crew if I left." Emotions warred on the navigator's face as he glanced from Edward to Lady Teresa and back again.

"Worry not about us. Ye have trained Fernando very well in the art. He be ready to take his place as a navigator. We be fine." Edward leaned closer to Henry and whispered, "Remember, ye be able to see Lady Teresa and continue your friendship."

"But Edward, you saved my life when you rescued me from the other ship. I am deeply indebted to you. I don't feel right about leaving."

"Henry, ye have paid the debt many times over. Ye not be owing me anything. I do hope that we continue to be friends, and that we be seeing each other when the Falcon is in port here."

"Of course, I would come to see you, Edward. Is this what you really want?" Indecision warred with hope on Henry's face. Edward knew he had made the right decision.

"Aye, Henry. Ye be a young man, and ye need a different type of life. One that gives ye the pleasure of a wife and, hopefully, many children."

Henry happily shook Edward's hand, then turned to Alphonso. "Sir, I would be happy to accept your offer."

Lady Teresa clapped her hands and ran to Henry, where she fell into his arms. Tears of happiness streamed down her cheeks. Alphonso shook Henry's hand, welcoming him to the new position.

"A toast!" Norman brought out the bottle of Scotch.

After the whisky was eagerly quaffed, Alphonso declared that it was time to get back to their ship. They would be leaving tomorrow at first light.

"I'd like to say goodbye to the crew before leaving off," Henry told Edward.

"That be good, Henry. I be staying here a little longer to visit with me brother before returning to the ship. I be wanting to see you before you go." Edward clapped Henry on the back. He'd be sad to see his navigator go, but he knew the man had a joyful future ahead of him.

"Ready to leave, Millie?" Alphonso asked.

Millie wrung her hands and glanced at Edward, hoping he would help her out of her predicament. Seeing her hesitancy to say anything to her employer, Edward turned to Alphonso. "Millie would like to stay on board the Falcon for a while. She has enjoyed sailing to the various islands and living the vibrant Caribbean life."

Alphonso smiled and shook his head. "I thought she might wish to stay. Edward, it looks like we have made a trade. I get a navigator, and you get a wonderful, bright young lady." Turning to Millie, he said, "Millicent, you have been a loyal helper and friend to Lady Teresa. I understand you are at an age where you want to experience more of the world and feel you would be in safe company with Edward. I know Lady Teresa will miss you, and I further want you to know that if the seafaring life does not agree with you, you are free to return to your job at any time. Good luck, my child, and enjoy your adventure."

Lady Teresa ran to Millie and hugged her. "Millie, I will think of you every day. If you are able, please write to me while you are on your travels."

"Lady Teresa, I will yearn for the days we have had, but I will also rejoice in my new adventure. I know we will see each other again and rekindle our friendship. Thank you for always being so kind to me. Tell Sophia that I will miss her also." They were both laughing and crying at the same time.

The two hugged again before Alphonso told the group that they must take their leave.

As the others left, Norman invited Edward and Millie to tea to spend a little time with his niece and nephews. Edward was in agreement, and they left the offices for a short trip to the family manor house. He had a wonderful visit with his family before heading back to the ship, where he would reluctantly say goodbye to Henry. They had been together for almost three years. Edward knew he would miss the camaraderie of his friend, but he knew Henry was making the best decision for his life. At least Edward had Millie. Her companionship would assuage his loneliness.

The next morning at dawn, the Spanish galleon carrying Alphonso, Lady Teresa, and Henry sailed south to Seville. The

Falcon left port shortly after, not wanting to take any chances with local authorities, and sailed west to the Caribbean Islands. As the ship sailed through the smooth seas, Edward and Millie stood at the bow of the ship, watching the water part for the handsome brigantine. They were quiet for a time, each lost in their own thoughts.

Then Edward turned and kissed her forehead. "I dinnae know what be in front of us, but I want ye to know I be very happy ye be with me. I dinnae know how long our time together will be, but I do think that joy be with us all the days we have together."

He took her in his arms, pulled her closer, and kissed her as the rising sun climbed high enough to turn the low morning clouds into glowing flames of orange, blanketing the muted brightness of the early sky. As he released her from his kiss and held her close, he knew the feeling of the fiery passion of a thousand burning suns.

∽

*K*ate saved her work and hesitantly closed the computer. The reality of the draft being finished gave her an overwhelming sense of melancholy. She attributed it to the fact that after fleshing out the storyline and editing the manuscript, she would be leaving the new friends she created. She did not allow the thought of the true reason for her sadness—the knowledge that Edward was sailing away with Millie. They would share their life and love together in the beautiful islands.

Chapter Nineteen

Kate hurried to the theater to meet David and start their second practice session. When she told Casey what happened, Casey had been sympathetic about the problem created by Marco and was more than happy to have David in the competition. Yesterday had been the first real practice day. Kate was amazed to discover that she and David were perfectly synchronized in their movements and steps. Having that knowledge made her even more excited. Tonight was the night, and she felt that they were as ready as they would ever be. As she turned the corner to enter the theater, David was coming towards her, smiling broadly and looking excited to start the final practice.

Casey set up the sound system and gave the remote to David, so he could start and stop the music as needed. The Charleston was their first dance. To add a little interest to their performance, they had agreed to use Marco's original plan of starting from different sides of the stage and dance towards the middle, where they would come together for the quick, kicky steps.

The first few strains of the music began. She and David took the first steps in quick unison as they moved effortlessly across the stage. As they came together, he took her in his arms, and they began the fast toes-in, heels-out twisting movements. He showed his expertise, effortlessly leading her through the steps. They soon fell into a perfect, harmonious rhythm. Since he had plotted out the dance before the first rehearsal, the steps came easily, and they glided through the routine. She was happy to see that they still were reading each other's transitions perfectly and were able to go through the whole dance without missing a step. Even the iconic knee and hand crossing went off without a hitch. As the song ended, he gave her a high five and a big hug.

"I don't know if I told you, but you are one of the best partners I've danced with in years." He beamed at her. Kate was thrilled and hoped the tango would go equally as well.

David had selected "Jealousy," a popular song from the 1950s for the tango. The drama of the music provided a well-suited background for the sultry, sensual dance. They ran through the routine several times, since the timing was critical, and there was more showmanship necessary to convey the mood of the movement. He had chosen the Argentinean style of the close embrace dance, where couples connected either at the chest or hip area, which meant a lot of body touching body.

At their first practice, Kate had been a little self-conscious being that close to David, but as they danced, she relaxed more and let the music—and David—guide her mind and body. After running through the dances, they continued to work on some of the more difficult steps in each routine. They were so immersed in the practice they lost track of time.

"Time's up." Casey came into the theater and smiled. "Sorry, but it's time for the crew to set up the stage for tonight's performance. Can't wait to see you two on stage tonight!"

Kate and David left the theater tired but happy with their session and even more excited for the contest that night.

They went back to their rooms to get ready for the last formal evening of the cruise.

From past cruises, she knew this night would be special, with an amazing dinner followed by the dance contest and ending with the captain's party. She was a little nervous about the dance contest, but she knew with David beside her on the stage, any apprehension would disappear.

She took her dress out of the closet and carefully slipped it over her head. She had chosen a high neck pleated satin cocktail dress with an asymmetrical hem and smocked waist. The indigo color accentuated the blue of her eyes and contrasted beautifully with her silver hair. She completed the ensemble with a long necklace of round, symmetrical Tahitian pearls that had been her grandmother's. As she slipped on the necklace, she heard Ellie come into the room.

"Wow, Grandma! You look beautiful."

"Right back at you. I love that dress and the way you look in it."

Ellie had selected a V-neck, knee-length chiffon cocktail dress in emerald green. She was wearing the ring Kate had given her, and her hair was done up in a French twist with wispy tendrils framing her face. Kate always admired her granddaughter's physical beauty, but it was her inner beauty that she enjoyed the most.

"Are you nervous about the dance contest tonight?" Ellie asked.

"No, not really. I'm probably more excited than nervous. We had a great practice yesterday, and then today, we polished everything up and concentrated on the technical aspects of the dances, like the hand movements and facial expressions, just the finishing touches that really add to a performance. But I was completely surprised yesterday during practice at how quickly David and I were able to read each other's signals and fall into a rhythm. It almost seemed like we had been dancing together for years. I never knew college professors could be as good on the dance floor as they are in the lecture hall. I wonder what other talents he has?" Kate laughed. "I'm really looking forward to the performance tonight. I don't care if we win anything or not. Just taking part in the competition has been so much fun, and that's enough of an award for me. So, are you ready to get this night started?"

"You bet." Ellie opened the door, and the two headed to dinner and the beginning of what promised to be an exciting evening.

As they entered the dining room, Kate saw the others had already arrived. She couldn't help but notice how handsome David looked in his black tux and deep-green cummerbund. His salt and pepper hair was pulled back into a low pony-tail. His beautiful green eyes sparkled when she approached the table. Again, she couldn't help but compare David and Edward. The similarities between the two appeared more obvious tonight.

The men stood as the two women took their seats. Kate had never seen such an attractive group of dining companions before. Oscar and Adam also wore tuxedos, and Amanda was dressed in a beautiful retro Victor Costa iridescent taffeta cocktail dress that she said she had won in an auction sponsored by a charity in their hometown. The shimmering fabric changed colors as the light above played against the folds of the skirt.

The dinner special was lobster thermidor served with a brandy sauce, oven browned Gruyère, and steamed asparagus. Everyone at the table opted for the special. After ordering, the group eagerly began discussing the night's events.

"I don't know what I'm more excited for—the dance contest or the captain's party," Oscar said. "Maybe the dance contest. But only because I can't wait to see you win and crush that little cockroach Marco in victory!"

Kate laughed. "I am quite sure Marco will not be in attendance tonight."

"Your victory is still his loss," Amanda said. "And that guy deserves a thousand losses."

Kate smiled, grateful for the support. "I doubt that my dancing skills are up to par for the win, but I'm having a lot of fun anyway. I think the captain's party will really be something to see. Those are always extravagant."

"I can't wait to see the champagne waterfall," Amanda gushed, bouncing in her seat. "It's so magical to see all the glasses stacked and filled! It seems like they should all just topple over, but they don't."

Kate looked around the table at the wonderful new friends she had made. It was satisfying to know they would stay in contact after the cruise since Adam would be living in Austin, and Kate knew Oscar and Amanda would visit him fairly often. Plus, Kate was quite sure Adam and Ellie would continue their friendship.

David mentioned he would like to visit her and view the stars in the blackness of the night sky from her patio. Kate thought the viewing of the stars was just an excuse to see her, but she was glad to have his company either way.

Ellie looked entirely smitten with Adam, which only increased Kate's wonderful feelings for the way this cruise had turned out. What an amazing ending to a remarkable two weeks.

She was drawn from her thoughts when the dining staff began parading through the large dining room waving napkins and loudly singing. This was the beginning of the goodbye performance for the guests. She both looked forward to the evening and was saddened by the departure of her wonderful new friends.

The lights dimmed, and all the staff stood by their assigned tables as they sang a song based on *Hello, Dolly!*, but the words had been changed to goodbye my friends. After the song, they began the Macarena, and guests joined in the dance. Everyone either clapped along with the music or waved napkins above their heads. Adam and David joined the dancers and demonstrated their prowess at keeping up with the hand movements while deftly moving their hips in time with the music.

The dancers then formed a dance line that circled around the dining room until everyone was back at their original spot. The audience cheered and clapped for the dancers as the spotlight moved towards Casey, who was approaching the middle of the room with a microphone in hand.

"Just a reminder, the dance contest will start in one hour." Casey paused to let the applause die down. "Conserve your energy so you can enjoy the exciting performances. And before you go, I have a new cow joke for you. How do you count cows in a field? With a cowculator!" The audience good-naturedly groaned in response.

As the festivities wound down, people began saying their goodbyes and making their way to the promenade deck for more pictures before heading to the theater. Kate and David told the group they would meet them in the theater after the contest. They slowly moved through the crowd on their way to get dressed.

The dressing room was a flurry of activity as Kate entered. She took her costumes off the rolling rack and went to a vacant fitting room to change into the fringed flapper dress. Thankfully, Casey had chosen regular heels instead of stilettos. Kate wasn't sure she could even walk in stilettos much less dance a fast dance like the Charleston in them. She walked over to a dressing table with a mirror and tried on the Marcel waved wig that went with the 1920s costume. After making sure the wig was securely fastened, she picked up the makeup bag she had brought with her to dinner for tonight. She made short work of cleaning her face, then carefully applied foundation and powder for a youthful glow. Smoky eyeshadow, black eyeliner, and black mascara made her eyes look larger. The brow pencil matched the hair to the wig. She topped the look off with blush and a red lip contoured into the perfect cupid's bow. With the addition of the feathered headband, she was confident she looked the part.

Kate left the dressing room and saw David standing backstage. He looked wonderful. His black suit and shirt suited him well. He had slicked back his beautiful wavy hair and adapted a rather gangster expression. As she walked towards him, he smiled and gave out a low wolf whistle. "Kate, you look sensational!"

Thrilled with the compliment, she graciously replied, "You look pretty good yourself." She glanced at her watch. "I think it's getting close to starting time. We are the second number, so I guess I'll walk over to the other side and be ready when they announce us. Hopefully, I won't make us fall on our faces." She laughed nervously.

Before they parted ways, David gave her a quick kiss on the cheek. "You'll be phenomenal."

The first dancing couple was already there when she approached the side of the stage. She smiled as they waited for the show to start. Soon, they heard Casey's voice welcoming everyone to the contest and excitedly introducing the first couple, who would be demonstrating a waltz. As the lights dimmed and the music began, the dancers entered the stage. With continuous flowing movements, they circled the floor in the rise and fall action of a waltz.

Watching them, Kate felt her first moments of apprehension or, perhaps, sheer terror. This was not a practice dance; this was real. She wasn't sure she was ready. As the waltz ended, the couple took their bows and quickly left the stage amid loud applause. Casey walked onstage to congratulate the first dancers.

Okay, old girl, this is it, so just smile and hope for the best. The internal pep talk did little to calm Kate's nerves.

"Ladies and gentlemen, we have a treat for you tonight," Casey continued. "Author Desiree Desire and Professor

David Mitchell will demonstrate a dance from the Roaring Twenties that made the flappers flap. Let's give it up for Desiree and David dancing the Charleston!"

As Kate heard the first few notes of the music, she put on her best smile and entered the stage with fast-paced steps timed perfectly to David's, who entered from the other side of the stage. Even though the spotlights kept her from seeing the crowded theater, she could feel the excitement in the air from the honky-tonk jazz sounds of the ragtime piano and the crying wah-wah of a muted trombone. The audience began to clap in time with the music, as if they too had been caught up in the upbeat rhythm.

Exhilaration coursed through her body as she moved in perfect harmony with David and the lyrical beat of the song. This was magical! Gazing into his eyes as they drew closer together only added to the moment. A slight tremble passed through her body. She could think of no one better to be dancing with than him.

They began the toes-in, heels-out twisting steps and swinging arm movements. She could feel his hand on her back expertly guiding her through the precision leg kicking steps and body twisting that were part of the iconic dance. As they turned to face the audience for the knee and hand crossing moves, she could see the sparkling reflections of light from the disco ball overhead as it slowly turned in circles.

She was no longer afraid, completely caught up in the moment—the music, the dance, the audience, and most importantly, David. Everything was perfect. Happiness overflowed in her, and she was thrilled to take it all in.

As suddenly as it had started, the music stopped, and the dance was over. David took her hand, and she twirled to face the audience and bent in a low curtsey. She then turned to David, who bowed to everyone before the two turned and ran off stage waving as they left.

Backstage, Kate laughed as she listened to the appreciative audience, clapping and yelling. Standing by David, she leaned on his arm, reveling in the moment. He put his arm around her and drew her close.

"That was wonderful, Kate! You danced like a pro. I don't think we missed a beat. Plus, I still have all my toes, and no bruises on my legs." He winked at her. "I call that a successful performance. If we can just keep the momentum going for the tango, we might have a chance to win a trophy!"

Kate wasn't sure about the trophy, but she knew they had done their best. She was glad she hadn't made a complete fool of herself on the stage. *Now, if I can just get through the tango.*

The couple headed to the dressing rooms to get ready for the next dance. Kate changed costumes as quickly as she could manage and left the room. David stood in the offstage area, dressed all in black. The clothes fit well over his still muscular body. His longish salt and pepper hair had been changed from a ponytail to a slicked back man bun that gave him an air of mystery and intrigue.

She smiled as she approached him. "You look very handsome."

David looked her over admiringly. "And you look very seductive and beautiful."

They took their positions near the stage and watched as the couple onstage finished their dance. His hand held the crook of her hip, giving her comfort. Applause resounded as the couple onstage bowed and walked off. During practice, David had suggested that they start the routine with a touch of Adagio and then go into the seductive close steps of the tango. Casey had told them the stage would be set up like an Argentinean cafe, and there would be small tables and chairs circled around center stage with some of the regular theater cast members seated at the tables for realism. David and Kate soon heard applause as the dancers left the stage and the curtains closed. Immediately, the stage crew began bringing cafe tables on stage and a tall bar stool, which was placed in the center of the stage. The stage took on the look of a cafe, just as Casey had told them. Several crew members took the empty chairs, waiting for the dancers to come on stage.

Despite his reassuring touch, Kate still had butterflies in her stomach. "I hope I don't step on your toes."

As soon as Casey announced their act, Kate walked on the stage and perched on the barstool with one leg extended to her side, revealing the long slit in her skirt, which she thought had gotten even higher. There was no turning back now.

The stage lights dimmed. The curtain slowly opened, and a spotlight aimed just at Kate. As soon as the audience saw her, they began to clap appreciatively.

The energy in the theater made her feel connected with the crowd. The first strains of music floated throughout the auditorium. David entered the stage and moved to stand behind her. He placed his arms on her elbows and slowly slid them up to her shoulders. She stood and began to walk away when David reached for her and pulled her close to his body. They began to sway with the music and move with the close, exaggerated steps of the dance.

Kate playfully pushed him away and turned back to the barstool. He turned and began to walk away. Seeing that he was leaving, she stood quickly and ran toward him. He turned to face her, and she leapt into his arms, wrapping hers around his neck. She then slowly lowered one leg and stretched it out behind her while David held the other against him as they twirled to the music.

The crowd went wild, clapping furiously. The Adagio start to their dance was over. She lowered her leg, and the two began the close steps of the tango, characterized by long pauses and difficult, stylized positions. As they danced in the traditional circle, she twisted and turned, using dramatic head snaps and high kicks while she gracefully intertwined with David's movements. Their bodies swayed together in faultless harmony. He expertly guided her throughout the dance. The sensual music and the excitement of the crowd were almost tangible. She let the energy flow through her body as she lost herself in the moment.

One hand in his, she twirled around him with twisting quick steps, then threw herself against his chest. She clung to him, arms loosely around his neck, allowing her body to slightly lower as she arched her back, bent her right leg and extended her left leg out in one smooth, fluid motion. He wrapped his hands around her back to hold her and leaned his head down close to her, striking the dance's final pose.

They held the position until the music came to a close. Kate felt her body relax, her lips parted as she looked into his eyes, shining and soft with desire. There was a rush of warmth in her body, and a tingling sensation ran through her as David drew her even closer. She could feel his breath getting heavier, and she could see a faint flush in his cheeks. Still in the pose, David suddenly leaned down and kissed her passionately on the lips. The audience cheered wildly. He quickly stood and, without looking at her directly, took her hand. She faced the crowd and curtsied, and he bowed. They waved as they ran off stage.

Backstage, he stopped and took her hand, looking at her apologetically. "I'm so sorry about the kiss. I guess I just got caught up in the moment. I hope I didn't offend you. I should never have kissed you without your permission."

"You're sorry you kissed me?" She was confused by his sudden apology. She'd quite enjoyed the kiss and worried that he regretted it.

"No, no! I'm not sorry for the kiss at all—just the way I handled it." He ran a hand over his hair and shrugged. "I should have asked you for permission first."

Kate leveled her gaze with his. "I liked the way you handled me," she said boldly, full of confidence from their sensual tango. "But I do need to give you a gift in return." Saying that, she leaned up and kissed him soundly on the lips.

David laughed and pulled her into his arms for an affectionate hug before they left to change clothes in anticipation of the awards announcement. As they walked backstage, she could hear Casey talking to the audience. "How about that tango?" She paused as the audience roared in response. "Wow, I don't know whether I need a cold shower or a cigarette. It may take both to get over that, and I don't even smoke!" The crowd broke into laughter. "Okay, in a few minutes, we will have the judges' decision on the winners of the dance contest, but first, you have to hear a little joke. What do you call a cow lying in the grass?" A pause. "Give up! It's ground beef!"

The audience gave the expected groan and laughed at the joke. Casey was known for her cow jokes. A few in the crowd had heard this particular one more than once.

Kate and David changed back into their regular clothes while the judges made their decision. The couple walked on stage with the other contestants and anxiously awaited the results. After what seemed like an eternity, the curtain finally opened. She grabbed David's hand as Casey began to speak.

"Ladies and gentlemen, we have the results, although the judges had a difficult decision due to the superb talent all of our contestants brought to the competition. Let's give all of them a big hand for their hard work and wonderful performances!"

The audience roared its approval and clapped loudly.

"Okay, it's time to find out who the judges chose. Third place in this year's dance-off goes to Pat and Paul Peterson from St. Louis for their beautiful rendition of the waltz. Let's give it up for Pat and Paul!"

Loud applause and whistles resounded throughout the theater, as the audience showed their appreciation while Pat and Paul stepped forward to take a bow and collect their trophy.

"For second place, the judges chose Mimi and Elmer Beckett from Macon, Georgia, for their lively 'Boogie Woogie Bugle Boy' jitterbug!"

Again, the audience clapped and cheered for the couple, as they walked up and graciously accepted their trophy and waved at the crowd.

"Now," Casey continued, "the award for first place and winner of a seven-day cruise of their choice, goes to a couple who demonstrated in both of their dances that seniors still have some moves left in them. And from their steaming hot tango, they still have a lot of other things left in them, too! Our own celebrity author, Desiree Desire, and her partner, Professor David Mitchell, from Austin, Texas!"

The crowd gave them a standing ovation, clapping wildly as Kate and David stepped forward to collect their trophy. The couple turned to face the audience, holding their trophies over their heads and rejoicing in the moment.

"Desiree, WE LOVE EDWARD!" The screams came from several women seated in the balcony.

Kate looked up in the direction of the voices and loudly yelled, "And from what I know about Edward, he is ready, willing, and able to love each of you in return!"

The crowd immediately broke into laughter and more applause.

"Thank you everyone for joining us tonight. A special thank you for the contestants and judges for their participation and making tonight a huge success." Casey paused to let the crowd cheer some more. "Don't forget about the pirate party the captain has specially planned for you in the atrium. We have real pirates joining us tonight, so have your cameras ready."

Chapter Twenty

*A*s the theater cleared, David and Kate walked out to meet their waiting group. When they got close enough, Ellie ran up to her grandma and hugged her. "Grandma! You were fantastic! I didn't know you could jump like that. That was aggressive!"

Kate started laughing. "I didn't know I could jump like that either."

Oscar and Amanda congratulated them, equally as surprised at how physical the dances were and how well they were executed. Adam grinned and said to David, "My favorite part was when you kissed Kate. Man, you planted a good one on her!"

David looked a little embarrassed and mumbled something about thinking the kiss added emphasis to the performance.

"Yeah." Adam gave David a light elbowing in the ribs. "That's your story, and I'll bet you're sticking to it."

They all had a good laugh and headed to the atrium. As the elevator doors opened on the upper floor, there seemed to be pirates everywhere. Even the female crew members were dressed as pirates as they walked among the guests with trays of champagne.

"This looks like a scene straight from your book, Kate," Amanda remarked as they made their way into the crowded room.

"Edward would feel right at home at this party." Kate took a glass of the proffered bubbly and walked over near the dance floor.

"A toast to a wonderful cruise!" Oscar raised his glass, and the others followed suit, clinking them together. They spent the first few minutes discussing the night's events and the wonderful experiences they had enjoyed on the cruise.

After a second glass of champagne, Adam asked Ellie to dance. Oscar and Amanda left to walk out on the deck to watch the waves break against the side of the ship.

"After all that dancing, I'm famished. Care to join me for a snack?" David held his arm out to Kate, who took it.

"That sounds perfect."

The couple ambled over to the hors d'oeuvres area and filled their plates with boiled shrimp, salmon rolls, mini pizzas, and other tempting treats. Taking their plates, they moved to one of the tall bar tables, where they could stand and eat while discussing the contest.

"I can't believe how good we were." She took a bite of a salmon roll. "Well, I can believe how good you were. I can't quite believe I was able to keep up with you."

"Nonsense, Kate. You practiced for days and earned that win. You don't give yourself enough credit."

Kate smiled but didn't have anything to say to that. In an effort to change the subject, she said, "So I guess it looks like we're going on a seven-day cruise together."

David shook his head. "You don't have to take me, Kate. Take Ellie. It's your prize."

"We won it together. It wouldn't feel right to take the prize all to myself." She paused, hesitating before continuing, but the boldness of the night had stuck with her. Something about the way they moved together gave her confidence with

David. "Besides, I wouldn't mind spending more time with you. A week-long cruise together sounds nice."

David smiled at her, eyes twinkling with delight. "I would love to, Kate."

They ate their appetizers in comfortable silence until their plates were empty. She looked around the room, considering whether she wanted another helping. As her eyes roamed across the various platters, she scanned the room until they landed back on David.

He stared at her, smiling. It had been a long time since she'd seen any man look at her like that. Not even Marco had ever treated her to such a smile.

With a sigh, she shrugged her shoulders. "I guess the only thing to do now is decide where our ship-on-a-stick trophy is going to end up: your trophy case or mine?"

David laughed. "Academics don't get many trophies, so I'm not sure where I'd put it. Feel free to add it to your collection." He reached across the table and took her hand in his. "Kate, I can't tell you when I've had so much fun. This cruise has been wonderful and most of the wonder has come from you."

She smiled demurely. "I have had a fantastic time, too. I'm so glad we were all seated together for dinner and that we have had the chance to get to know one another. Oscar and Amanda both have wonderful senses of humor, and Adam couldn't be nicer. I know Ellie is glad she met him. It's funny how things work out." She looked out on the dance floor over at Ellie and Adam, then turned her attention back to David. "When we got on the ship, I was having issues coming up with some type of plot for my novel. I had no idea I would meet people as wonderful as all of you." She squeezed his hand. "Now, I have the manuscript outline completed, we all have plans for after this cruise, Adam and Ellie are going to continue to see each other, and you and I can continue our friendship. I hope."

David kissed her hand. "I think it's more like you won't be able to get rid of me."

Standing there, each became lost in their own thoughts. Kate reflected on the day with a relaxed contentment. This cruise couldn't have worked out more perfectly. The storyline of her book was completed, they won a dance contest, of all things, and she'd met someone who was not only real, but a person she was beginning to care about. All in all, a pretty good vacation.

While they stood at the bar quietly watching the dancers and listening to the music, something caught her eye. It couldn't be. It just wasn't possible, but there he was walking towards her.

"Kate, you look like you've seen a ghost." David's concerned voice penetrated her stunned mind, but not enough for her to respond.

She couldn't form the words to answer and kept staring across the room. The tall, handsome pirate walked towards her, dressed in the authentic clothing of an eighteenth-century pirate. His dark wavy hair hung neatly down to his shoulders. His confident stride gave him the demeanor of someone who was used to being in charge. It was the brilliant green eyes focused directly on her that stole her breath away. She knew those eyes.

Upon approaching them, the pirate asked David, "Kind sir, would ye be in favor of me asking for a dance with the lady?"

She could feel David's gaze upon her, but nothing could tear her eyes away from the pirate in front of her.

"I don't have an issue with you dancing with the lady, but this lady makes her own decisions. It might be better if you ask her yourself."

Edward turned toward Kate and softly asked, "Would ye do me the kindness of having a dance with me?"

Kate continued staring without saying a word. It was as if she forgot to speak, so lost in the unreality of the moment. She was barely aware of the announcement by the band-leader. "We have a request from one of the pirates who wanted a special song played for his lovely lady. So, let's slow the tempo down just a few beats to let everyone enjoy a romantic dance with their special person. Let this be a night you never forget. This is an oldie but goodie from years ago. Join us for our rendition of 'Lonely Wine' sung by our own Jennifer Owens."

The lights in the atrium dimmed as the first strains of the music flowed through the air. Still speechless, she slowly took the pirate's hand. He led her through the crowd to the dance floor. As she turned to face her partner, she glanced through the windows and saw nothing but a heavy fog. The low lighting and blanket of white encompassing the ship was like walking in a misty dream. Other dancing couples faded into the background, leaving Kate and her pirate the only two people in the room. It was as if they had crossed over into another realm of existence, one that was not based in current reality but reflected its own warm and exciting setting. A setting that made her feel young, vibrant, and attractive.

Standing on the dance floor, the pirate turned and took her in his arms. As they drew together, the closeness of their bodies sent a shudder of heat through her. She finally managed to whisper, "Edward, how? I mean you have never visited me while I was awake, and you never have revealed yourself to any other person. I don't understand what is happening."

Edward gently pulled her to him, bringing up a long-buried longing inside her. She nestled her head against his shoulder. This was her Edward—the one she created and gave life to. The one who had visited her for years in her dreams and laughed with her as they argued over plots. The same Edward who could drive her crazy with his stubbornness but who was always there during her times of need. Their friendship had grown deeper in recent years. While she knew he didn't exist, she couldn't imagine what her life would be without him. Now that she was in his arms, she wanted to touch him, to breathe in his scent, to taste the ocean salt on his skin. The melodic sound of his broad Scottish brogue gently kissed her ears. She had never stood this close to him before and was surprised at how tall and muscular he was. Her whole body came alive as the music drew them even closer.

"Aye, Katie girl. This be an enjoyable cruise, but the time draws near when we be parting." He leaned his face against her cheek as he spoke. "Ye have David now, and I be sailing to the islands with Millie, but I could not be leaving without the chance to have one dance with ye. One chance to hold ye in me arms and feel the softness of yer body next to mine; one chance for our souls to come together as true lovers."

Kate moved her hand up to his neck and drew his other hand close to her breast. She could feel the tautness of his muscles and the strength in his arms. She tentatively moved her hand up the back of his neck to touch the beautiful curls that framed his face. As her fingertips glided over his skin, she once again felt the electric tingle of desire run through her. She knew Edward could feel her passion. His breath was heavy, and he looked into her eyes with a palpable longing. They danced silently as the music continued to encircle them, keeping them close together while the lyrics validated their longing.

"Katie girl, I don't know how or why we be brought together, but I do know that we be destined to spend eternity as lovers. There be no other woman who has made me feel that way before ye. The past years we be together be the most wonderful of me life. Ye be a warm, loving, and beautiful woman. Ye be the quiet place; the calm within me swirling sea. Ye have shown me all the things that I never thought to see, and ye possess the serene face and peaceful grace of me stability. If perchance, ye should falter, I want to be keeping ye safe and nourish ye within me. Ye be me inspiration, the tenderness of me salvation. Through ye comes the simplicity of all life's sanctity. Ye be the meaning of me existence. I long for the time when we be joined in our shared reality."

Kate was overcome with emotion from the poetic beauty of his words, but at the same time, she was confused by his love for her. "But Edward, I'm twice your age. I don't understand why you want me when there are so many other younger and prettier women that you could have."

"As I be saying, in the existence of me life, there be no age. When I look into your eyes, I see a beautiful, spirited, and passionate woman. I see the soul of ye, and inside the soul is where love lives."

Tears clouded her vision as she felt the depth of his emotion mixed with the soulful music encompassing her body and mind. Their bodies swayed in unison as they held tightly to each other, fearing the separation that the music's end would bring. She felt the dizzying effects of the champagne coupled with a soaring, powerful passion. She tried to rationalize the moment. This couldn't be happening. She couldn't really be dancing with Edward. But, locked in the embrace of their dance, she knew without a doubt that the man holding her was very real. He had awakened feelings in her that she had kept buried for a long time. With alarm, she heard the last lonely words of the song. The end was here. She didn't want the music to stop. She didn't want to go back to drinking her lonely wine.

As these thoughts raced through her mind, she lifted her face to his and leaned in to kiss him, but he took her face in his hands and gently kissed her on the forehead. His voice full of sadness, he said, "Aye, Katie girl, if I be feeling the warmth of your lips on mine and the closeness of your body locked in a lover's embrace, I dinnae think I be able to leave. This not be our time yet, and until that time comes, I will think of ye every day and dream of the moment when we be meeting as lovers, and I can finally be touching ye and holding ye close to me as the woman me heart will love forever. Time not be a factor in all existences. Remember what I be telling you, Katie girl." Edward leaned down and lightly kissed her forehead.

She murmured, "I do remember, Edward, and the thought of those words makes me very happy."

The music had stopped. Their time was over. She was hesitant to leave him, but he gently laid his hand on her arm and walked her back to David.

"Thank ye, kind sir, for allowing me the pleasure of a dance with yer lady. She be a fine woman, and I hope that ye take good care of her."

"I definitely will take wonderful care of our lady, Edward. I will take care of her for both of us."

A fleeting surprised look came into Edward's eyes as he heard David call him by name. Smiling, Edward reached out to shake the other man's hand. "Ye be a good man, Professor David Mitchell."

"Thank you, Edward. I wish you clear skies, smooth sailing, and following seas."

Edward took Kate's hand in both of his, then gave her hand a kiss and said, "Katie girl, I be seeing ye in a few months to work on our next book."

He smiled at them and started towards the deck exit doors.

Kate stared after him, unable to wrap her mind around what had just happened. He paused at the deck door and waved before fading into the fog. David and Kate stood looking at the door, neither saying anything. Finally, he turned to her and said, "I don't know what just happened, but I'm going to chalk it up to an exhilarating night, three glasses of champagne, and a little fatigue setting in."

Kate laughed lightly. "I like your explanation, and as Adam said earlier, that's our story, and we're sticking to it."

As they were getting ready to head to their staterooms, Oscar and Amanda approached them.

"Who was that gorgeous pirate you were dancing with?" Amanda asked. "He looked just like the image I have of Edward from your books."

Kate secretly winked at David. "Oh no, Edward isn't quite that good looking. I think he was just one of the crew that Casey sent to dance with me as a joke."

"Well, I wish I had someone who would send me a pirate like that, as a joke or for real!" Amanda exclaimed.

Oscar looked at Amanda and laughed. "What do you mean? You've got me and I'm real!" Turning to the group, he continued. "This has been a great party. We were out on deck, and I could have sworn I saw an old brigantine sailing ship anchored close to our ship, but the fog rolled in, making it difficult to get a good look. The cruise line really went overboard in planning this party!"

David and Kate replied in unison, "Yes, they did!"

Chapter Twenty-One

*L*ying in the bed in her stateroom, Kate's mind went to the events of the evening. She could not remember a time when she had been a part of such an exciting night. The dance contest could not have worked out better. David's kiss had been a total surprise but was the perfect way to end the dance. She'd gladly have him do it again.

Again, she was amazed at how much Edward and David were similar in appearance. While she had thought that before, seeing them together made the likeness more evident. They were both about the same height and weight. They both had shoulder-length, wavy hair, and beautiful green eyes that could penetrate to the very core of a person. They both had that same sparkle of warmth in their eyes.

Romance might have come late in her life, but when it did, it slammed into her like a train. She had not one but two men in her life—one based in reality, and the other was literally the man of her dreams. *How this plays out is going to be very interesting, Miss Katie girl!*

With those thoughts, she fell asleep with a satisfied smile.

The next morning, both Kate and Ellie slept in a little later than usual. All the excitement and activities from the night before gave them an excuse to lounge in their rooms until their stomach made a request to find food. She glanced at her watch and saw that it was almost 10:00 a.m. She crawled out of bed and made her way to the shower, where she hoped the steaming water would make her ready to face the day.

As the gentle massage of the pressure from the water stroked her neck and shoulders, she thought about how the last day of a cruise was always a little bittersweet. They had been gone for two weeks. While she was excited to go home, the cruise had been so much fun. Leaving her new friends would be difficult.

Perhaps they could find a way to get together over the holidays. Amanda had mentioned that their older boys and their families could only come for Christmas, which aligned with Kate's family traditions. Thanksgiving might be a good option for all of them. She could invite Amanda and Oscar to stay with her for the whole week. She thought about all the places they could visit during their stay. Amanda would enjoy the Texas Olive Company and maybe a drive to Fredericksburg to see the Christmas lights in the town square. David and Oscar would probably just follow along and do whatever the girls wanted. The two men got along so well that Kate imagined they could just relax and talk somewhere in one of the craft breweries or wineries that were springing up all over the Hill Country. Yes, that would be a wonderful Thanksgiving, made even better with David there.

At eleven, Kate and Ellie headed up to the lido deck for a late breakfast or early lunch and to meet the rest of their group. As they entered the dining room, the normally high energy room was a little more subdued and laid back. Individual groups of new and old friends sat together, taking pictures of each other and trading contact information. What a beautiful time of peace and friendship.

As they walked through the area, someone called her name. "Kate, over here." She looked around and saw David standing by a large table by the window. She and Ellie hurriedly joined him.

"How did you get such a great place? Window tables are at a premium," Kate said. "I have never had luck getting one, and you got a table large enough to seat everyone. Good job!"

"I would like to say it was a feat of bravery and excellent skill, but actually, I was walking through the door when I caught sight of a couple of people standing up at the table and others putting their napkins down and gathering their belongings. I just ran over and stood by them until they felt compelled to hurry and leave. There are times when being obnoxious pays off."

Kate laughed. "David, I don't think anyone would ever find you obnoxious. They probably just wanted to leave quickly so you could be comfortably seated."

As Kate and Ellie took their seats, Oscar, Amanda, and Adam came walking over.

"Wow!" Oscar exclaimed. "Who found this table?"

"The stargazer took his eyes from the heavens long enough to grab us a wonderful place to eat and enjoy the water," Kate said.

"All of you go ahead and get your food. I'll just sit here and watch the waves while I hold the table," David said.

"You don't have to tell me twice," Oscar joked, rubbing his stomach. "I am so hungry I could eat two or three brunches."

With that, they all headed to the omelet bar for the first course.

After everyone had gotten their food, they sat comfortably at their window table, enjoying their last delicious breakfast.

"I've had a wonderful idea." Kate leaned forward to share with the group. "Thanksgiving is in three weeks, and I thought it would be a wonderful time for us to get together and celebrate the holiday as a kind of reunion. I'll happily offer my home to everyone. There's enough room for all of us. Adam, Ellie, and David will already be in Austin, so Amanda, you and Oscar are welcome to drive over and stay in the guest casita for as long as you like. I'll only have Ellie for the Thanksgiving holiday, since my children and other grandkids won't come until Christmas. If any of you have other family members that might like to come, they would be welcome."

Amanda gasped then smiled. "Actually, our other boys don't come for Thanksgiving, so I think it would be great to be with all of you again. Without Adam, there would have been only the two of us. Frankly, I was wondering what we could do this year and whether it would even be worth cooking a turkey for just the two of us. I think this is a wonderful idea." She looked over at her husband and nudged him lightly in the ribs. "If the boss here says yes, then we would love to come to your home."

"Ha!" Oscar laughed. "The so-called boss agrees with Amanda. I think that is a banner idea. Thank you for the invitation!"

David smiled. "Count me in. I haven't had a good home-cooked Thanksgiving dinner for a few years now. Chinese food has been my best friend."

Kate and Amanda spent the rest of the time planning the menu, while Oscar and David discussed what football games to watch. Ellie and Adam had their heads tipped closely together, no doubt making their own plans to see each other much sooner than Thanksgiving.

The rest of the day passed slowly. Oscar and Amanda returned to their cabin to pack and get ready for disembarkation the next morning. Ellie and Adam spent their last day in the pool, and Kate and David went up to the upper deck to watch the water and sip a little frozen liquid refreshment.

She had been sad earlier because this was the last day of the cruise. She had thoroughly enjoyed this cruise and hated to see it end. However, knowing everyone would be getting together later in the month diminished the earlier sadness. And while she didn't want to admit it, she was thrilled by the knowledge that David would be visiting.

The water was especially beautiful. The waves gently broke on the side of the ship and spread a blue-white foam out to the side, forming a pathway that slowly disappeared as the large vessel silently glided through the deep waters of the gulf. They sat together in a comfortable silence, just enjoying the experience. The warm sun beamed down, but the breeze was cool enough to keep the temperature comfortable. After finishing their drinks, they sat back on the couch, lulled by the gentle sway of the waves. Before long, both had drifted off into a relaxed sleep, with Kate's head resting on David's shoulder and her hand laying snugly in his.

He woke first and kissed her on the forehead. His soft touch woke her. She looked up and smiled warmly at him and squeezed his hand. It was so good to feel this kind of happiness. David was everything she had dreamed of for so many years. He was kind, gentle, intelligent—and real!

"Wake up, sleepyhead," David whispered. "It's almost time for us to get ready for dinner."

"Okay, but do you think we could devise a plan to hide in the lifeboats tomorrow and stowaway on the next cruise? I'm really not ready for this cruise to be over."

He laughed as he stood up and reached for her hand again. "That wouldn't be a bad idea, but I'm afraid the others would miss us, and we would become the object of a huge manhunt, resulting in embarrassing headlines when we were finally discovered sleeping in a lifeboat, or sneaking food from the lido deck. Face it, my dear lady, we are destined to leave the ship in the morning."

"If we must," she playfully sighed as he gently pulled her up from the couch.

"Kate! Wait up a minute." She turned to see Casey excitedly rushing towards her. "I've got some good news. I've made arrangements for your group to have an escort meet all of you in the lido dining room around ten in the morning. They will accompany you as you collect your baggage and go through customs. The ship's hotel manager didn't want to risk you meeting up with Sam and Betty when you disembark."

"That is very nice, but really, I had not even given Marc... uhh, Sam a thought in days."

"I'm glad, but we felt bad that you had the unpleasant experience while you were a guest here on our ship. We want to make sure we make your final moments on ship as great as possible."

"It's not necessary, but I really appreciate your thoughtfulness. We will be happy to have an escort accompany us when we leave." Smiling warmly at the young lady, Kate said, "Casey, you have made this trip memorable. I hope to be lucky enough to have you as a cruise director the next time we travel. You are funny, lively, and full of charm. All the qualities needed to be a successful cruise director. I plan to write a letter to the cruise line's corporate offices to let them know how great and caring you were to all the guests."

"Thanks, Kate. You and your group have been wonderful guests. If you'd like, I can send you an email once in a while and let you know what exotic places I have been sent to."

"I would like that very much. I like to keep in touch with the nice people I meet in my journeys. Thank you for all of your help!" Kate hugged the young lady who had made her dreams come true by asking her to be in the dance contest.

Chapter Twenty-Two

The group met for their last dinner. The dining room wasn't as crowded as usual, since a lot of people opted to eat at an earlier time so they could get ready for their travel home in the morning. As usual, the waiters were very attentive. The group soon had appetizers, baskets of bread, and drinks as they waited for the main course. Everyone had chosen the surf and turf entrée and tres leches cake for dessert. The meal was wonderful. Conversation centered around Thanksgiving plans and an Alaskan cruise planned for possibly the next year, after Adam and Ellie had been at their jobs long enough to get vacation time.

"We would be open to a short Caribbean cruise in the spring, Kate. That is, if you and David would be interested," Amanda said.

Kate laughed. "I do believe we have a couple of cruise converts here. I'm always ready. I would just have to check my schedule as the book should be ready to launch in early spring. If that works out, I'm in. David?"

"If it could be timed to coincide with spring break, I'd love it!"

They soon finished the dinner and dessert. There was a sad happiness that filled the room as everyone thanked the dining room staff and their table servers for their outstanding service. An announcement paused the conversations. "It's time for one last dance."

The "Macarena" began playing, prompting an eye roll from a handful of guests. But everyone was soon patting their shoulders and twisting their hips as they all took part in the last show of the cruise. Hearing the song reminded her of how lucky she was. Even the Marco fiasco served to bring her and David together. If Marco hadn't taken her dancing and Casey had not asked them to be in the competition, then Kate wouldn't have had such a fantastic experience or David's passionate kiss.

Soon, it was all over. Guests slowly filed out of the dining room. Kate and her companions returned to their staterooms to get their luggage outside of the rooms so that the crew could begin picking up all the baggage to get it ready for tomorrow. They all hugged and said their good nights after agreeing to meet on the lido deck at 9:00 a.m. for breakfast before they left the ship.

Kate opened the door to their suite and entered, followed by Ellie, who sat on the couch in the sitting area. After a couple of minutes, she exclaimed, "Wow! This has been the best time of my life. I don't know of anything that could have made it better."

"I totally agree. We've made new friends, people who will probably be in our lives for a long time. We saw wonderful sights, and the first draft of my book is finished. I am one happy lady." Kate smiled and sat down beside her granddaughter.

"Does David have anything to do with your happiness?"

"David was the icing on the cake. I wasn't even thinking about the possibility of romance, but then he was there. A real, live man for me to enjoy."

"Grandma, there is something about David that reminds me of what Edward would be like if he were older. I've read your books and listened to your stories about Edward visiting you, so I feel like I have a good idea of what his personality is, and David just seems to share some of the same qualities. He even has the long wavy hair and beautiful green eyes. It is a little strange."

"I noticed that the first night we all met at dinner. It was odd, and the fact that Edward was so adamant in his repeated warnings to me about Marco seemed a little out of place. He kept telling me that David was the right man for me."

Ellie smiled. "You mean the right man, since he can't have you, right?"

Kate sighed. "Maybe. You seem to have found a man for yourself too."

"I hope," Ellie said, blushing. "Adam is sweet and funny. On all our adventures together, I never felt unsure or embarrassed. I never thought about how he was seeing me at any given moment. I just felt comfortable. It was nice to be around a man who didn't make me feel like I had to be someone else."

Kate wrapped an arm around her granddaughter and squeezed. "He seems very nice. I'm glad you found someone who treats you the way you deserve."

"Thanks, Grandma. He really does. What are the odds that we both found love on the same cruise?"

"Probably minimal." Kate laughed and shook her head. Ellie yawned next to her, and Kate knew they couldn't delay the end of their fun any longer. The cruise was ending, whether they went to sleep or not. "Elle, you better get to bed. Tomorrow is going to be a hectic day. It'll be nice to have Adam going back with us. Do you think he would mind if I asked him to drive? That way, I can sit in the backseat and reflect on our wonderful vacation and not have to worry if you are falling asleep while driving."

Ellie grinned and leaned over to kiss Kate's cheek. "Grandma, thank you so much for this trip. You couldn't have given me a better gift, although the ring was pretty nice too."

"I'm glad, Elle. That makes me very happy. Good night, ladybug."

"Night, Grandma."

Kate woke before dawn the next morning. She always liked to sit on the balcony and watch as the ship slowly made its way past refineries and other factories as they entered the waters along Galveston Island. The morning was cool, and there was a slight breeze. She leaned back in the lounge chair, alternately dozing and enjoying the solitude.

"Kate. Ye be almost home. Have ye had a good trip?"

She looked up at Edward standing beside her. She was immediately struck with the memory of their dance together and felt closer to him than ever. "Edward, I didn't expect to see you today. Oh yes, this has been a remarkable vacation. I don't know when I've had so much fun. And I finished the first outline draft of the book, so now I'm off to flesh it out for the editors. I thought you were with Millie at your island home."

"Aye. I wanted to see ye again before ye were off the water. Ye be the same as me; we both belong on the open sea, sailing by the stars, marveling at the colors of the morning sunrise and evening sunsets. We both be happy listening to the sound of the waves rising and falling as the ship cuts a path through the ancient waters. The rocking of the ship is like the mother's rock of a wee cradle. Kate, ye be a true seafarer, and I love the way ye change when ye be in your proper element."

"You are right, Edward. I do so love being on the water and the peace and serenity the oceans bring. I would have loved living on a sailboat and sailing around the world with the man I love. But I stayed at home and created a wonderful family. My life couldn't be more filled with love than it is now."

"I be happy for ye, Katie girl. I now must leave and go back to the *Falcon*. I be coming to visit after the book is published to see how it fares with the people. I also be having some ideas about the next adventure. Take care and be happy with David." He leaned over and kissed her forehead as he slowly faded from view.

She continued to doze on the lounge chair as the ship slowly kept its course to the Galveston Cruise Terminal. It wasn't long before she felt the bump of the large ship being tied to the dock. They were back. The trip was over. Now it was time to go back to her home and the responsibilities that came with being a human being. She silently said a prayer of thanks for the wonderful vacation and the beautiful world that was given to the inhabitants of this fantastic planet.

The group met at 9:00 a.m. for their breakfast. Everyone was looking forward to getting back to their individual homes. Even when vacations were above expectations, there was something so nice about being home. Promptly at ten, two crew members came to their table to escort them through the disembarkment and through customs. Everyone quickly stood up and walked with their escort off the ship to the baggage area and customs. Just as quickly as it had started, they were back on land and ready to board the shuttle that would take them to their cars.

Everyone shook hands or gave hugs one final time. David said he would call Kate later that evening, ostensibly to make sure they got home okay, but she knew he was going to be lonely after having the group around him for the past couple of weeks. She would miss his warm and comforting presence but knew they'd get together soon.

She at least had Ellie to keep her company while she waited for the next time she could be with David. Since Adam agreed to drive, he and Ellie sat in the front seat. Kate happily crawled into the back and buckled up for the five-hour drive home. As they traveled down the interstate, she comfortably relaxed and began replaying the whole vacation over in her mind, dwelling a little longer on the parts that included David and Edward.

Chapter 23

One Year Later

Kate heard the front door open just as the phone rang. She saw that it was her publicist, Sally, calling and picked up the phone just as David came into her office. She waved at him and mouthed "Sally" while pointing at the phone. He relaxed in one of the overstuffed chairs and began checking his phone for messages while Kate continued the conversation. After a few minutes, she shrieked into the phone.

"Sally, you can't be serious. You scheduled a meeting in New York just before Christmas?" She looked at David rolling her eyes as she pointed at the phone. She then put the phone on speaker so he could hear both sides of the conversation.

"That's right," Sally continued. "Oprah is doing a special on the accomplishments of older women in different fields of work that will air on March 8 for International Women's Day. Since you'll be in New York next month discussing the upcoming book tour, one of the morning shows wants to interview you as a teaser for the special. I think they are doing four individual segments, featuring a cardiologist from Chicago, either Meryl Streep or Helen Mirren, a professor from Harvard, and a bestselling author."

"Why would they use me for the teaser? Wouldn't it be more impactful to use one of the four women they are featuring?"

"Well," Sally paused. "They kind of are."

"I don't understand. Who else is going to be there?"

"No one, Kate. You are the bestselling author, and you are going to be interviewed by Oprah! They are going to do it remotely from your home and will send a member of their staff out to check the location and go over everything they will need for the show. This is such sensational news. I have been bursting with excitement to tell you after I heard from Oprah's program director. I am so happy for you. This will be a huge boon to the sales for the fiery passion book and also give you the recognition you deserve."

After a very long moment of silence, Kate finally was able to speak. "Sally, I am in a total state of shock. Being interviewed by Oprah is something that people don't even dare dream about. Who would ever have thought that an aging Desiree Desire would ever get her fifteen minutes of Oprah fame just because she's old? It's just surreal. I know that the first books of the Passion series reached bestseller status, but most of my other books did too, and I've never been interviewed."

"It's timing, Kate. Older women are in the news now. We are finally coming into our proper place in society and are valued for the contributions we have made and are continuing to make to the world. You give so many people happiness through your books, and Edward has now become a popular romantic hero to women around the world. People want to see you and discover for themselves how an older woman still can write with passion about the adventures of a thirty-eight-year-old pirate and the needs women have for true love and not just sex."

"I'm really fired-up about this interview. Thanks for letting me know. This is beyond exciting. Oprah! Wow! Maybe double wow! Sally, you have just made my day, no, my year. I'm sure we'll be in touch quite frequently in the next few months. Talk to you later." Kate stood there a minute after she hung up the phone, then she threw her hands up in the air and screamed. "Oh my gosh! I'm going to be on Oprah!" Laughing, she collapsed on her office couch.

"David! Did you hear what just happened? I'm going to be interviewed by Oprah for her special!"

David took her in his arms and kissed her forehead. "I'm so proud of you. You deserve all the recognition you'll get."

"Thank you, David. I'm still in a state of disbelief. This has been so unexpected, but so appreciated, that it is difficult to process what is happening." Suddenly, she almost shouted, "Oh my gosh! I've got so much to do to get ready for the interview. I haven't a thing to wear. I need to make some updates to the den, if that's the room they choose—and Thanksgiving is next week!"

He grinned down at her with a look of pride on his face. "Calm down, we have plenty of time."

"David, there's never enough time. Let's start making plans! I really can't get over this!"

The Friday after Thanksgiving, her caretakers, Carlos and Rosita, began putting up the Christmas decorations, and by the following Sunday, the house had been transformed into a Christmas wonderland. There were twinkling lights outside and fully trimmed trees and other decorations filled up all the common rooms inside. Kate loved the main Christmas tree since many of the ornaments were ones that were on her family tree when she was a child. She also loved baking

Christmas goodies and always included the worn recipe for her grandmother's bourbon wrapped dark fruitcakes. She laughed as she remembered that Ellie used to tease that she put more of the whiskey in her glass than she did when she wrapped the cakes in bourbon-soaked cloths for storage. Kate was inclined to agree with her.

The days passed quickly and soon Kate and David were headed to New York. Where had the time gone? This afternoon they would be in New York, and tomorrow, she would be at the Barnes & Noble location on Fifth Avenue for a reading and book signing. Friday morning, she would be at the CBS studios early in the morning for the interview about the upcoming Oprah special.

"This is a dream come true." She took David's hand as the United flight began to pull away from the jetway. "Here we are on our way to New York, two weeks before Christmas, and the weather report this morning said there was a light snow falling. What could be more perfect?"

His eyes glistened as he looked at her tenderly. "I'm so glad you are getting this opportunity. You've earned it."

She squeezed his hand and laid her head on his shoulder. It reminded her of the first time she did this, on accident, and she smiled, thinking of all the times she'd done it since. "I'm so glad we decided to stay a little longer and see some of the city. I hope it's not too cold to visit the open-air holiday markets and Radio City Music Hall. I also want to spend time at Rockefeller Center, watching the ice skaters skating around the huge tree, and walk down Fifth Avenue looking at all the holiday displays in the windows there. There's just so much to do in the city at Christmas. What do you want to see?"

"Mostly the normal tourist attractions, but I would like to go to the One World Observatory. I've heard the view from the top of the building is spectacular. I think we are going to be a couple of tired tourists by the time we get back home."

Kate snuggled up closer to him as the plane took them to their wonderful adventure.

Epilogue

"Katie girl. Be ye asleep?" Kate heard the voice come as if in a dream.

"Edward! Oh Edward. I'm so glad to see you. It seems like it has been such a long time since you were last here."

"Nay, I be here just a couple of months ago. Ye just be having very much going on in yer life that it seemed to be a long time. How be the trip to New York?"

"Edward, it was wonderful. The interview went well, and the city was beautiful. It was just like I would have written it if I were describing it in a book."

"Be ye happy with David?"

She smiled and nodded. "Yes. David is wonderful. He is thoughtful, loving, interested in what I do, protective—everything a woman could want in a man. You were right when you said he was a good match for me."

"Aye, in the life ye live now, he be perfect."

"How are you and Millie getting along? Is she still happy with a life at sea?"

"Aye, she be saying she be happy, but I think there be times when she misses her friends and way of life she had in Spain. But we be enjoying me home. There seems not to be so many ships on the seas now. Things be changing, Kate, and I not be knowing how the life of a pirate will finish. It may be time for me to leave the water and return to London to work with me brother, Norman."

"That may be the plot for a future book if we continue our series, maybe the final book," Kate responded.

"Katie girl, I be glad to see ye looking so happy. You be the type of woman who needs love in her life. David be good for you. I feel a little envious of the fact that he be able to have you as his love, but it be the right time for both of ye. When our time comes, I promise that I be doing everything in me power to keep ye as happy as ye be now."

"Edward, I truly don't understand what you mean by our time coming. Our real lives are three centuries apart. I don't think there would ever be a way we could live in the same time." Kate was beginning to drift off into a deep sleep.

"Time not be a factor in all existences. Remember what I be telling you, Katie girl." Edward leaned down and lightly kissed her forehead.

She murmured, "I do remember, Edward. Someday belongs to us."

The End

Acknowledgements

I am eighty-five years old and have just achieved a seventy-year-long goal. I wrote a book! As a young girl, I wanted to be a writer, but life and laziness just kept interfering with my plans and there was always "next year." At age eighty, it became pretty obvious that my "next years" were getting pretty limited and I better get moving if this would ever happen. Just writing the book was a major accomplishment but having the opportunity to have it published was more than I could have ever dreamed of. What I have discovered during this adventure is that books are never realized by just one person, and I want to recognize the wonderful people who have helped me on this journey.

First: I want to thank TLC Book Design for coming up with a beautiful cover that perfectly summarizes the meaning of the story. They were helpful, patient, and very supportive.

Second: A thanks to Misti Moyer, my editor, who was the most thorough person I have ever met. She made suggestions and corrected my mid-20th century grammar with the eye of an eagle.

Third: I have seven grandchildren and I want to acknowledge them on motivating me to continue on in this life. They have even gifted me with three great-grandchildren. However, there is one who shares my love of writing and is a talented free-lance writer under CBK Creative – Cadie Krivoniak. Cadie was with me every step of the way, critiquing my work, making suggestions but always telling me that it was my story, and I should write it true to my beliefs. She provided the necessary support and confidence that kept me glued to the computer. She is truly my ladybug of good luck.

Finally, there is no way this book would ever have been written if I had not had the good fortune to meet someone eleven years ago who not only became a web client but also a friend – Loren Steffy. Loren is an awarded journalist, has written five nonfiction books, and released his first novel, *The Big Empty*, last year. Through Loren, I became associated with the reality of the writing process and how words can be combined to tell wonderful stories. Loren is such an accomplished writer that in our discussions, I was hesitant to tell him of my dream of someday writing a book. When I finally off-handedly mentioned that I wanted to write a travel blog for seniors, he was right there telling me to do it. That produced *The Graytripper* website. As time went on, we talked a little about my dream of being a novelist and even though he said I should try, I still lacked the confidence and was falling back on my excuse of "next year." A little over a year ago in one or our emails, Loren casually mentioned that he hated something with the "passion of a thousand burning suns." I replied that his comment sounded like the title of a romance novel with swashbuckling pirates and lusty damsels. His response was: "write it." That was it – he had thrown down the gauntlet that spurred something in me to get moving and *Someday Belongs to Us* was conceived. Throughout the whole process, Loren was encouraging and motivated me to keep going. It was not easy to harmoniously string together over

65,000 words and come up with the logical progression of a story, but I persevered and here we are. There is no doubt in my mind that if I had not met Loren Steffy, there would not be a book.

And… to my readers, thank you very much for choosing my novel. I hope you love the characters as much as I do and that you get pleasure in reading about their adventures and misadventures along the way. Hopefully, this is the first of a trilogy and we will be meeting again with book two.

About the Author

Margie Seaman is an eighty-five-year-old, late-blooming author of her debut novel *Someday Belongs to Us*. After a forty-year career in marketing, she switched to a new venture in website design where she has been the president of Citation Solutions for the past fourteen years. Margie also writes a travel blog for seniors, *The Graytripper*, that encourages people to get out and explore their world. Margie is the mother of three, grandmother of seven, and great-grandmother of three. She holds a bachelor's degree from the University of Houston and lives in Houston, Texas, right down the street from her childhood home. She is currently dogless for the first time in her life but does have some totally spoiled cats that ungraciously allow her to share their living environment.

CPSIA information can be obtained
at www.ICGtesting.com
Printed in the USA
BVHW040358110522
636632BV00002B/2